Chasing Boys

Chasing Boys

karen tayleur

Walker & Company
New York

First published in Australia in 2007 by Black Dog Books
Published in the United States of America in 2009 by
Walker Publishing Company, Inc.
Visit Walker & Company's Web site at www.walkeryoungreaders.com

For information about permission to reproduce selections from
this book, write to Permissions, Walker & Company,
175 Fifth Avenue, New York, New York 10010

Library of Congress Cataloging-in-Publication Data
Tayleur, Karen.
Chasing boys / Karen Tayleur.
p.   cm.
Summary: With her father gone and her family dealing with financial problems, El
transfers to a new school, where she falls for one of the popular boys and then must
decide whether to remain true to herself or become like the girls she scorns.
ISBN-13: 978-0-8027-9830-5 • ISBN-10: 0-8027-9830-6 (hardcover)
[1. Interpersonal relations—Fiction. 2. Self-confidence—Fiction. 3. High
schools—Fiction. 4. Schools—Fiction. 5. Fathers—Fiction.] I. Title.
PZ7.T21149Ch 2009   [Fic]—dc22   2008023241

Printed in the U.S.A. by Quebecor World Fairfield
2 4 6 8 10 9 7 5 3 1

For Toph
A bOy who chased me until
I caught him

"I know **what** you want," said the sea witch. "It is very stupid of you, but you shall have your way, though it will bring you much SORROW, my pretty one."

—Hans Christian Andersen, *The Little Mermaid*

1.

Coop told Kelli Luong who told Meg Piper who told Desi Walczak who told me—Eric Callahan was going out with Angelique Mendez.

Definition of a rumor: when someone tells someone who tells someone else who tells someone else something that you may or may not want to hear, something that may or not be true.

2.

If I were talking to Leonard, which I'm not, I would ask him a question.

"Leonard," I would say, "what sort of person makes up a rumor for the sheer pleasure of making someone else unhappy?"

Then Leonard would look at me and clear his throat and do that tapping thing with his foot and I would get so annoyed that I wouldn't stay around for his answer.

That's the trouble with Leonard. He's just so damn annoying.

3.

It is true.

My trusted source, Desi, has confirmed that Eric Callahan is going out with Angelique Mendez.

And why wouldn't he?

See, there are two kinds of girls in this world. There are the in girls and there are the rest of us.

Angelique Mendez is an in girl. She has long black hair that could star in its own shampoo commercial.

Angelique Mendez has the body of a model, the voice of a rock star (she's always the lead in the school play), and the brains of a surgeon.

Angelique Mendez is the girl voted most likely to do whatever the hell she wants to before her twenty-first birthday.

Angelique's dad is a journalist and word is that Angelique is hoping to follow in his footsteps. No one doubts she will get there.

It had only been a matter of time before Eric and Angelique collided like two shiny comets in a galaxy of drab dead planets. I'm just surprised it took them so long.

It is Angelique and Eric.

Eric and Angelique.

I always hoped it would be Eric and El.

4.

I met Eric on my second day at Blair High School eighteen months ago. I was at Blair because my mother couldn't afford my old school. I don't know why she bothered to find a new school. All I wanted to do was stay in bed with the comforter over my head and listen to music.

Mom had chosen Blair because of its good reputation for twelfth-grade results. If you knew Blair you'd wonder how this miracle occurs. It's a school built for six hundred students and bursting at the seams with just over twelve hundred. There are temporary classrooms everywhere. There is a temporary classroom perched on the edge of the track. The outside basketball court has been completely taken over by them. There are classes held in rooms that should be condemned. Some of the desks still have inkwell slots. And the school is Multicultural with a capital *M*.

At my old school, Regis, you'd find me listed

under "exotic," because of my Mediterranean background. Dad's parents were Italian. My grandpa died before I was born and I can barely remember Nonna, who lived with us when I was really little. My sister, Bella, remembers her more. She says I have Nonna's dark eyes. So there I was, exotic girl at Regis and just another one of the crowd at Blair. I haven't bothered to count the number of different nationalities here—there are too many.

With the lack of facilities, it's hard to believe Blair is one of the top ten public high schools, but there you go. Maybe the teachers are really dedicated. Maybe someone is fudging the twelfth-grade results.

Anyway, Mom did her homework and I ended up here.

I was standing in the hall trying to work out the timetable, annoyed that I was going to be late for class. The last of the stragglers bumped past me like I was a piece of furniture. I didn't belong. My state-imposed uniform was so new it still had its original package creases. I traced the line again from 1:40 p.m. across to math.

"Lost?" someone asked behind me.

I turned to see Eric Callahan. I didn't know it was Eric then. (Later, when I described him to Margot, she said, "Oh, you've met the school hottie.")

"I think I'm supposed to be in 34C—wherever that is," I said. I tried to sound like I didn't care, but the tremble in my voice wrecked the effect.

"New girl." He smiled.

I nodded.

"You must be," he said. "I know all the girls worth knowing at Blair."

Part of me was pleased that he thought I was worth knowing.

He herded me up one hall, then another. We didn't actually touch, but I could feel his presence.

"I'm never going to remember my way around," I said to ease the tension.

He touched my shoulder. "You'll be fine."

Then suddenly we were standing in front of a door. 34C. It was shut.

"Great!"

Eric peered through the hall window into the class, then opened the door and walked in.

I followed behind like a puppy.

"A lost student for you, ma'am," he said.

He gave me a smile that warmed me down to my feet and then he was gone. The entire female population of the class sighed. Possibly not only the females.

And that's when I knew—you know—that

it was him. He was the reason I was going to get out of bed each morning. He was the reason Blair wouldn't be such a dud. He was the one who could make my day right, just by seeing his crooked smile at the lockers.

Eric Callahan was mine.

Until Angelique.

5.

When Desi confirms the rumor about Angelique and Eric we are in the library. We are in the self-help section for a change. I am looking for a book that will help me survive the whole Angelique and Eric thing. Desi has left to look for some tissues. She is taking it really badly.

I like to hang out in the library in winter. The winter wind blows at a 45-degree angle through the school's asphalt alleyways. It kicks up skirts, messes with your hair, and hacks at your bones like a blunt kitchen knife.

And summer isn't that much better.

Last year the school board ordered all trees—in fact, anything with foliage—be cut down to make way for more temporary classrooms. A small courtyard with a canvas roof is our only shelter from the sun during the recess and lunchtime breaks. Unfortunately, twelve hundred–plus sweaty kids crammed into an area meant for fifty doesn't work well. Math genius Eric Callahan could tell you that.

Eric Callahan is so good at math that he actually tutors other kids. He is like a roving Mr. Math Fix-it.

Am I talking about Eric Callahan again?

I usually hang out in the nonfiction area of the library with my best friends, Margot and Desi—usually around the biography section, because no one ever shows up there—and we try and keep it quiet until the end-of-lunch bell rings.

Keeping quiet is not always easy.

6.

Margot Blackman was the first person to talk to me at Blair. (The school secretary doesn't count.) I was sitting outside the office on a step, waiting for the morning bell to ring, when a girl with hard blue eyes and straight black hair marched up to me. I thought maybe I was in her spot or something, but she just glared and said, "Ariel Marini?"

I nodded.

"Mrs. Mackay told me to find you. You need to come to the main office for locker assignment. So we can do that. Or we could skip school and take in a movie at the mall. Your choice. I'm Margot," she said.

And somehow I just knew we were going to be friends.

Margot is tall and fragile-looking, like her bones might break if she bent the wrong way. In reality she's as fragile as a pit bull terrier. Her lips are a constant thin horizontal line. Margot never raises her voice above a bored monotone. Her best friend until I came to Blair was Desi—Desiree Walczak. (Desi's mother hated it when we shortened her daughter's name. She chose the name from some TV soap and thought it sounded very exotic.)

Now Desi is my best friend too. Unlike Margot, Desi can get quite excitable. She describes herself as a passionate person, but Margot says Desiree Walczak is a maniac, with bipolar tendencies. (Margot uses words like this when she wants to impress people. I was impressed, anyway.) It is true that Desi is either desperately happy or desperately sad, but I don't think that she's any different from other girls I've met. She's also quite pretty in a girl-next-door kind of way.

If we can keep Desi under control, the biography section of the library is ours. Apart from its being warm in winter and cool in summer, it's easy to smuggle in food, phones, and music.

Today is the first student newspaper meeting. The sign on the library door reads "Blair Newspaper— All Invited." Under the sign is a short paragraph: "Want to be part of the next school newspaper? Feel free to drop by. Meetings Mondays at lunchtime in the library conference room. Or give me a call." There is a phone number and a name. Angelique. Award-winning journalist in the making.

The glassed-in conference room is bursting with earnest-looking do-gooders, though not many earnest good-lookers. There are eight girls and three guys. None of the guys is Eric. I've seen a couple of the girls before. One of them is in my science class—Kat, I think her name is. Another, Meg Piper, is in my homeroom. I don't know two of the guys, but the third is a star on the school's basketball team—Coop. Angelique's newspaper group is made up of a Group of Nice Young People. This is what my mom would call them if she ever met them.

"Why don't you make friends with that Group of Nice Young People," she'd say.

Mom often capitalizes words.

It's not that Mom doesn't like Margot and Desi, but she's worried that I've only made two real friends at Blair in the last year or so. It's just that I don't see the point. I'm not staying here long. As soon as our finances get sorted out, I'm back to my old school. The one with the grass. And trees. Lots of trees. Angelique Mendez would not stand out at my old school.

Desi still hasn't come back with the tissues, and my bet is she's been distracted and is doing something else. I check out some books with one eye on the student newspaper session while I wait for her. Margot finds me sitting cross-legged on the floor, surrounded by books like *Self-Help for Nightmares* and *The Complete Idiot's Guide to a Healthy Relationship* and *123 Robotics Experiments for the Evil Genius.*

"So," says Margot.

"So," I say.

"It's not like the guy dumped you," says Margot.

This is what I like about Margot. She's the kind of friend who'll tell you how it is—even when you don't ask for it.

"I know," I say.

"I mean, you've been dreaming about him since last year, El. You've had your chance to ask him out or something."

This is the thing about Eric Callahan—I never had any intention of being his girlfriend. Or holding his hand. Or asking him out. I just wanted to know that he was there and available. Eric was my dream guy.

And I do dream about him. My daydreams have become pretty complicated. Sometimes they turn into different episodes where I leave off and pick up the story another day. Sometimes I change what happens in the end, sometimes the location, but always Eric is amazed that he hasn't noticed me before and declares that he can't live without me. It's pathetic really, in an incredibly satisfying way.

Of course, none of this makes sense to anyone else, so I just grunt like I agree.

"Best-case movie scenario?" asks Margot, sitting next to me.

This is one of our favorite games. Margot is convinced there is a movie scenario that fits every aspect of our lives.

We shuffle through the possibilities. I end up choosing *The Breakfast Club*, a favorite of Mom's. The story is about five high school students who meet one Saturday for detention. "A day that will change their lives forever."

"So you and Eric will hook up in detention one day, and he will finally see what he's been missing out on all this time . . . and he's gonna dump Angelique for you?" says Margot.

"Of course."

"I see a major problem with this plot."

"You do?"

"Eric Callahan will never get detention," Margot

says. "So you're gonna have to find a different movie."

"That's all I've got," I say.

"Maybe you could get Eric to tutor you in math?" suggests Margot.

"We can't afford it," I say. "Besides, I don't want him knowing how stupid I am."

Margot gives me a little push. "You are stupid, El Marini. Stupid for wasting your time. You spend your whole life dreaming. Maybe you should wake up."

Margot's tough love is not what I need right now, so I pick up a book.

Muted laughter rings out from the glassed-in meeting room.

"Maybe you should talk to Leonard about this?" says Margot, more gently.

I snort. Margot knows everything about me. Sometimes I wish she didn't.

7.

Leonard is a person I don't talk to once a week. I see Leonard once a week because of my father. My sister, Bella, says I have issues, but I don't think so. I just hate my father. Bella says Leonard's technically not a shrink, just some kind of "ologist," as if that makes a difference.

I spend my time in Leonard's office not talking to Leonard.

"Hello, Ariel," he begins.

When I don't answer, he writes down a few sentences in his notebook, then he spends the rest of the time sitting, looking out the window. I wonder what he's written, what he could write— *Ariel Marini, still not talking.*

Leonard lives in a part of town that used to be rich. All the two-story row houses look tired and dirty. The things that made them beautiful are falling off, or fading, or have gone. The street is narrow, built in a time where they could never have imagined the number of cars that would clog up the landscape.

It is the strangest thing, not talking to Leonard. Most of the time it is nearly peaceful. But sometimes he does something really stupid, and I just want to be at home under my comforter.

Two weeks ago, Leonard stopped looking out the window and leaned forward in his chair. "How do you feel, Ariel?" he asked.

How do I feel?

I'll tell you how I feel, Leonard.

I feel angry.

I feel hurt.

How do I feel?

I feel like someone has zipped me open and grabbed out my heart and said, Well you won't need that anymore.

I feel like I can't feel anymore. Like I'm walking and talking and sometimes even laughing, but inside I'm still and watching to see if I'm fooling anyone. Like I'm shoving food down my throat, but there's no taste. Like I'm screaming, but there is no sound.

Of course I didn't tell Leonard this. I just leaned forward and looked deep into his eyes.

"So, tell me, Leonard," I said. "How do you feel?"

He called Mom that night to say that we'd made progress. What a faker.

I pretend going to Leonard's is a game. I'm making up the rules as I go along. I am only seeing Leonard for now because Mom's been grouchy lately and this keeps her happy.

"Hello, Ariel," Leonard repeats.

I give him a short nod. Then I bang my school backpack—the one that Desi has graffitied all over with the name of our favorite band, Scheme—on the floor. Mom had freaked when she saw my school-bag covered in writing. She didn't understand when I explained that Desi was just expressing herself.

"Maybe she could express herself on her own bag" was Mom's reply. "That bag cost me fifty dollars."

But I like my bag. Scheme is awesome. They can be really loud and crazy, but their lyrics are amazing. They really get to where you live. I look down at my bag and wonder if I could sneak my earbuds in while Leonard isn't looking, but figure I can't.

I flop down on my seat near the window and sigh.

Leonard's office is opposite a park. Through the

window, the trees wave their little leaves at me but I don't wave back. The best thing about Leonard's office is the view of the trees. I love the way they are there. Whether I visit Leonard or not, the trees are there. They were there before I knew them, and they'll be there long after I stop seeing Leonard.

The heat purrs through an open vent. It's hypnotic. For a moment I imagine it's gas seeping into the room. Any moment now I will sink to the ground, never to wake again . . .

I should be so lucky.

Leonard sits opposite me, smoothing his pants and crossing his ankles. Then he clears his throat in a way that always drives me crazy. It's like he's just about to say something, but he never does.

Can I go home now?

I don't say this out loud, because I don't want to start talking to Leonard. Once I start talking, he'll start asking questions. I've seen it before in the movies. One minute the doc is asking you about the weather, the next he's asking you why you hate your father.

I pull my cell phone out and check the time. I have been here three minutes and forty-eight seconds.

I must really love my mother.

8.

My dream has just come true.

9.

Eric Callahan has ended up in detention. Just three days after Eric and Angelique became the school's hottest couple, Eric was caught cheating in the half-year math exam. The half-year math exam is where ninety students get to sit together in the gym and worry about what will become of the rest of their lives.

Of course, it was a mistake. Eric is good at math. It's just that Desi, who had been advised for the past four months that she could take a cheat sheet into her math exam, blew it. She'd taken the wrong page with her.

Desi was sitting, silently crying in the exam, her tears smudging the ink on her wrong cheat sheet (a page of scribbles she'd been working on just before the exam to figure out how much allowance she'd get over the next two years), when Eric handed her his sheet. Ms. Clooney caught him and sent him out of the room, along with Desi.

That's where my "knight in shining armor syndrome" (Margot's words, not mine) kicked in.

When Eric and Desi were kicked out of the math exam, I stood up and tried to explain the situation to Loony. ("Ms. Clooney" rhymes with "loony." It's such an obvious link that only the seventh graders call her this. Sometimes I resort to this because I never got to use it back then. Regis had its own special teachers.)

She told me to sit down and finish my exam. I kept standing and tried again. Then she offered me a chance to explain in detention the next day. Did I mention that Ms. Clooney was on my case? She was always going on about me not "achieving my fullest potential," so I'm sure I made her day.

That's how I ended up in the coffin room for detention with Eric Callahan.

It's called the coffin room because it has no windows—none that you can see through. At some point someone slapped chalky white paint over the glass. Apparently they used to show movies here, before our super-expensive (joke) school auditorium was built. Now it is just the coffin room—a dead end.

I'm sure Mom would be Very Disappointed if she found out I was in detention. Luckily there was no need for her to know. If there were a subject called Forgery One, I'd get an A.

Desi and I go to detention early, just to get a good seat. Also, I hate being late. Each desk has only one chair, so Desi takes the desk closest to me on my right.

My daydream about Eric is that it will be just like *The Breakfast Club*. Eric and I will spend an amazing long lunchtime in detention, where we'll get to know each other. Angelique is history.

Then Ms. Clooney walks in with a clipboard and a stack of folders and the daydream evaporates. She nods in my direction and sits at the desk at the front. A couple of other people shuffle in and sit down. Eric comes in and takes a seat by a white-painted window. He looks pretty relaxed. I peek at him from under my bangs, but he doesn't notice me.

Ms. Clooney takes attendance and notes that someone called Dylan is missing. I'm just wondering who this Dylan person is when a guy turns up, looks around, then heads to the back of the room.

"Up at the front please, Dylan," says Ms. Clooney. She sounds like she's just invited him over for coffee, but there is an edge to her voice that means business. She points to the desk next to mine.

Dylan slumps in the seat and glances at me. I realize he's the newest new guy at school and I give him my catatonic stare—the one I use when I want the other person to look away. It's usually pretty effective. He has a thin white scar, almost invisible, that travels from his bottom lip and disappears under his chin, and just for a moment I wonder how it got there. His lips curl into a sneer and I look straight ahead.

"Okay, everyone seems to be here," says Ms. Clooney. "Welcome to detention. I'm your hostess for this trip. There are no emergency exits. You will write me a five-hundred-word essay on a subject of your choice and hand it to me by the end of detention."

There are groans all around. Ms. Clooney is hilarious. She is a dried-up husk of a woman who hates her job and doesn't care if everyone knows. I wonder if she has ever laughed in her life.

"If you like, I can make that a thousand words."

Then she gets a tiny dark-haired girl to hand out paper. Most people have brought their pencils, but Dylan has nothing to write with. He stares at the blank paper until Ms. Clooney asks people without writing instruments—her words not mine—to get a pen.

Dylan strolls to the front desk and takes his time choosing a pen. Then he strolls back.

Desi gets straight to it. She writes like it's a race and she wants to be first over the finish line.

On my left, Dylan is balancing the pen on his index finger. I know his type. Bored. Macho. Thick. He looks at me like he's just read my mind and I hunch over my paper. But I don't write. I can't think of anything to write about.

I look over at Eric. His pen flows evenly over the paper and a lock of hair falls down over one eye.

My heart does its little Eric-melting thing.

Ms. Clooney is at the front, marking papers. A chair scrapes across the floor and it sounds like a fart. Someone snorts with amusement. Kids in the tiny yard outside our window are shouting and laughing. The clacking of high heels disappears down the hall. A door slams with a hollow thud. Someone calls out for Em, Em, to get back here.

I make a few doodles on the page, then write a heading—"My Vacation." I cross it out. Then I write, "An Injustice" and start to explain the injustice of Eric, Desi, and myself being in detention. I count my explanation and it only adds up to 167 words. With ten minutes of detention still left, Desi gets up and marches over to Ms. Clooney. She slaps the paper down in front of the teacher, then moves back to grab her coat. As she makes for the door, Ms. Clooney says, "Where are you going, Desiree?"

Desi points to her essay.

"I've finished," she says.

"Really?" Ms. Clooney scans the page in front of her while Desi shifts her weight from one foot to the other. "This is excellent," says Ms. Clooney.

This is not good.

"Excellent? Really?" echoes Desi.

This is one of Ms. Clooney's favorite games. I'm surprised that Desi doesn't recognize it. I call it the cat-and-mouse game.

Ms. Clooney is the cat. She raises her paw and Desi is surprised at her freedom. But Desi's freedom is an illusion.

I clear my throat loudly and raise my hand to distract the cat, but Ms. Clooney ignores me.

"Yes. It's a perfect description of last night's movie," continues Ms. Clooney. "I'm sorry, Desiree. I thought you understood. This is to be your own work." Then Ms. Clooney rips the page in half and throws both pieces into the garbage can next to her. You can tell she enjoys it.

My hand wavers in the air, then sinks like a slowly deflating balloon.

Desi stands in front of Ms. Clooney's desk with her coat. She still doesn't get it. She looks at Ms. Clooney, who has gone back to marking papers. Dylan continues to balance his pencil. Desi looks desperately at me. I jerk my head to the right, back toward her desk. Her shoulders droop slowly as understanding clicks in. She shuffles back. I hand her a spare piece of paper and she sits and doodles.

I can't get my injustice explanation to pad out to 500 words. It only takes a few paragraphs. That's the trouble with the world's injustices. They aren't that difficult to explain.

I decide to write a story instead. Each time I start, I cross it out. There is really no such thing as a new story. Finally the end-of-lunch bell rings and Ms. Clooney asks us to hand in our essays. Most students, including Eric, hand her something and leave. Eric passes Dylan's desk and they raise fists and knock knuckles.

"Hey," says Dylan.

"Hey," says Eric.

Eric gives me his Eric smile as he strolls out the door. I know he uses it on all the girls, but I can't keep my heart from tripping over itself.

Eric Callahan has noticed me. I must still be alive.

Eric probably has no idea he's the reason I'm here. I realize I'm staring at him and turn to find Dylan watching me watching Eric. I make a big deal about packing up my bag so I don't have to look at him.

There are only three people left who don't hand anything in. Dylan, Desi, and I are left without 500 words to show between us.

"Well," says Ms. Clooney, gathering her things together, "looks like I'll be seeing you three tomorrow. Same time. Same room."

She leaves and Dylan snorts.

"She . . . she's so . . . ," says Desi.

"A movie rewrite," says Dylan. "Nice work."

"How was I supposed to know she'd watched *The Night of the Living Mummies?*" mumbles Desi.

Something makes me think that Ms. Clooney hasn't watched *The Night of the Living Mummies*. But I don't say anything.

"I've never been in detention before," says Desi.

She sounds really sad, but I am not fooled for one second. Desi's doing that wide-eyed thing she does when she wants boys to notice how gorgeous her blue eyes are. Now she's doing the pouty thing with her lips. Desi would flirt with King Kong if she had the chance.

I leave her to it as I grab my bag and walk to the door.

"Hey! What's your name?" Dylan calls out.

I turn around to see him looking at me.

"Ariel," I say. No one calls me Ariel. No one except Mom. "Ariel," I repeat.

Dylan's lip curls again and he says, "Well, see you tomorrow—Ariel Ariel."

Something in the way he says it makes it sound like a promise.

10.

So how did detention go?" Margot manages to look bored and concerned at the same time as we scramble at our lockers for next period's books.

"You know." I shrug. "What did you do at lunchtime?"

"Same old. How's Desiree?" she asks.

"Still beating herself up. How it was all her fault that I was sent to detention. How she can never look me in the eye again. Blah, blah, blah."

Margot nods. "As long as she's feeling okay, then. How was your Eric? Did he thank you for coming to his rescue? Was it just like *The Breakfast Club?*"

Margot's expression is deadpan as usual but her eyes glint with something that looks like triumph. Triumph over what? was the question.

"First, he's not my Eric," I say. "Second, I didn't actually rescue him. He stayed in trouble and I just got myself into trouble. And third . . . let's just drop it."

Then we are in the middle of the hallway shuffle. Margot doesn't have a chance to reply and, frankly, I don't really want to hear what she has to say. Angelique is up ahead. The crowd parts before her as she makes her way gracefully through the sea of bodies. Eric's arm is draped casually across her shoulders.

I imagine it's me leaning into Eric's side.

Suddenly I want to be Angelique Mendez. I want to be her so much, it's scary.

11.

I keep a mental list of things to ask Leonard, in case one day I talk to him. I doubt this is ever going to happen but . . . well . . . stranger things and all.

I add Angelique to my list. I'd like to ask Leonard if it's normal to want to be someone else so much that you would lose yourself.

If it's normal to fantasize about terrible things happening to her so that you can swoop in and offer support to her grieving boyfriend.

If it's reasonable that you've already picked out your outfit for her funeral.

If it's okay that you study the way she walks and talks and smiles and flicks her hair and bites at her lower lip when she's concentrating.

And if it's strange that you lock yourself in the bathroom at home and part your hair in the middle, in that Angelique style, and suck in your cheeks to find your un-Angelique cheekbones.

Also I would ask him how much money my mom is paying him. How much he charges for a visit. Maybe I could make a deal with him. We could go in half and half on his fee and I wouldn't have to turn up anymore. It would certainly solve my nearly nonexistent spending-money problem and give him some extra time. A win-win situation. Mom wouldn't have to know.

But then I think of Leonard with his pressed pants and crossed ankles and know he wouldn't go for this.

12.

Second-to-last period of the day is geography and Dylan is in the class. He walks in unnoticed and sits at the back of the room. Desi is excited to see him again, but Dylan only shifts around in his seat when she gives him a little wave. I'm just glad Margot isn't around to see her.

When Desi and I have geography, Margot has history. Last year we were together for every subject, but this year it's changed. We still have our core subjects together—math and English—but our electives have split us up.

"Let's choose the same electives," Desi insisted at the end of term last year. "Make sure we have the same preferences."

We sat in the library one lunchtime and copied down the same electives and preferences—one to eight—but of course we all ended up with different schedules.

Geography's pretty boring, but our teacher, Mr.

Ray, is good. He's the only person who could make volcanoes and the salination of our waterways even vaguely interesting.

He spends most of the lesson explaining our "big" term project.

"I really want you to get your teeth into this, people. This is your chance to understand what's happening in your own neighborhood. We'll be looking at introduced vegetation, population density, traffic movement. The project involves a couple of field trips. I'll also be handing out a list of possible sources for extra research."

Desi leans into me and whispers, "Doesn't he know I only do it the night before it's due?"

"And don't think this is something you can do in one night," continues Mr. Ray. "Now, let's talk about teams."

I assume that I'll be doing the project with Desi, but Mr. Ray is writing down names on strips of paper, folding them, and putting them into an ice-cream container.

"I want everyone out of their comfort zone," he announces, "so I'm going to pull names out of a hat."

Desi looks panicky.

"But I want to do it with El," she says loudly.

The boys let out some hoots and whistles until Mr. Ray tells them to quiet down.

Mr. Ray pulls names out of the hat and writes down teams of three on the whiteboard. Desi's name is one of the first to be allocated and she has ended up with Christy, the quiet mouse, and Joel, the hood who's always trying to sell you something that came from a friend of a friend of a friend.

I'm feeling a little edgy as names are pulled out and teams are announced. When my name is pulled out along with Sarah's and Nathan's, I relax. Sarah, who I don't know that well, gives me a thumbs-up. But Nathan says, "I'm already on a team, sir."

Mr. Ray makes a show of scratching his head and assuming an "aw shucks" expression before wiping Nathan's name off the board and pulling out another name.

"Dylan Shepherd," he says, just as I knew he would.

I ignore Desi's nudge and write down the names in my notebook like I might forget them.

Sarah McVee, Dylan Shepherd, El Marini.

I don't dare look behind me to see Dylan's face.

"I want you to get into your groups now and work out a plan. You'll need to exchange contact details if you don't already have them. Our first excursion is two Tuesdays away, so you'll need to get organized quickly."

Everyone groans as they leave their seats and get into project groups. Sarah bounces over to Dylan. I slowly pack up my things and move over to them to hear her already organizing us.

"I was just telling Dylan that my weeknights are totally out. I mean, totally. If we're going to do this as a group, it's going to have to be on the weekend. So there's the field trip thing, with stats and stuff. I hate stats. Then there's the history section. I'm good at history, so maybe I should take over that part of the project, if that's okay with you?"

"Sure," I say.

Dylan nods.

"We can't meet at my house ever. I mean, never. I have two little brothers and they are totally loud. Out of control."

"So where—," I begin.

"Hey, great. Your place, El?" Then Sarah writes down her e-mail address and phone number on two neatly torn pieces of paper. She passes one to Dylan and one to me. "I can't make it this weekend, though. It's full. I hate it when they spring things on us like this. Do you have a computer, El? Scanner? Printer?"

I've got lots of computer equipment. It sits on a tiny table that used to be a hall table in our last house. But we don't have Internet access. Mom says it's a luxury we can do without. I don't mention this, though. I just nod and write down my details, including my address.

Dylan doesn't write anything, but Sarah is too busy to notice. She has launched into a debate on a PowerPoint presentation versus a professionally printed book when I peek at Dylan to see what he's thinking. He's looking seriously at Sarah, nodding every now and again, then he reaches over to me. I flinch, but he's just pulling a twig out of my hair. He turns back to Sarah, who seems to have a lot to say about nothing.

Then the bell rings and Sarah says, "So next Sunday at your house, El? Eleven's good for me." Then she strides away.

"I have some permission forms for your parents to sign or you won't be going on any field trips," says Mr. Ray. "Please take one on your way out. This is going to be fun, people."

I wait for Desi by the door. She nudges me as Dylan passes us but I ignore her.

"I don't want to do my project with them," she hisses as the rest of her group leaves.

I shrug.

"You hate me now. Because of detention. El, I'm sorry. Detention was horrible. It was all my fault."

"It's okay."

"If it wasn't for me you wouldn't be there."

"I was actually just trying to explain the situation."

"You're too noble," moans Desi. "If I were you I would never speak to me again."

Then I laugh at the thought of me being Desi. After a second, she joins in. Then she pulls out the latest Delia's catalogue from her bag and says she definitely has to have the top on page 22. She doesn't stop apologizing about detention until I promise to meet her at the mall in her quest for the perfect look.

"You realize it's Thursday night," she warns.

"You owe me big-time," I say.

13.

Thursday night is everyone-at-home-for-dinner night unless there's something else that's so important you can't get out of it. It always has been. Even after Dad was gone, Thursday nights continued, but with one less place at the table. Some nights we get to sit in front of the TV and eat dinner. These are my favorite nights. But Thursday dinners are spent at the dining room table.

There are certain rules in our house that never change. When you eat in the dining room, you must have a tablecloth. You must have a bread-and-butter plate out, even when there's no bread on the table. You must have a jug of water with sliced lemon and ice cubes and matching glasses on coasters. In a pinch, sliced oranges will do.

The best part about Thursday-night dinners is that Mom makes an effort and cooks something special. For the rest of the week it's quick stuff, but Thursdays we have a roast or some special

Italian dish that Mom's really good at, like gnocchi or eggplant parmesan. These are dishes that her mother-in-law, Nonna, taught her, and they have become family favorites.

Thursday-night dinners can be okay unless Mom is in detective mode.

Tonight we have an early dinner so I can go out to the mall.

"How was school today, El?" Mom asks.

It's always the same answer. I don't know why she bothers.

"Okay," I say.

"Anything exciting happen?"

"Nope," I say.

"Any tests?"

"Nope," I say.

"Any homework?"

"Done,'" I say.

"Any boyfriends?" chimes in my sister, Bella.

"Yep, five," I say.

Then Bella starts talking about college—she's doing a business degree—and I'm off the hook.

Sometimes Mom will tell us about her day. She works at the local Social Services office. Her stories mostly sound the same. Not enough funding. Old people needing more home care.

Young mothers needing day care. I don't know how she can stand working nine to five—nine to eight on Wednesdays—when for years she was just helping Dad out with his business. Import, export. Whatever that is.

Tonight I ask her if she misses her old life: driving around in an expensive car; meetings over lunch; being her own boss and all that. The silence at the table is punctured by the ice cracking in the water jug.

"No," she says briefly.

I'd broken the rules. I'd talked about how things really were instead of pretending that life was great and our life before never existed.

"'Did I tell you about my economics lecture today?" says Bella.

And I go to the kitchen and top up the water jug.

I'm sure that Leonard would be happy if I told him about Bella.

I'm sure he'd be happy if I just said hello.

Bella is my sister but we don't look like we belong together. Ever since she was four, she's had to be the older sister. Ever since I can remember, Bella has been there.

Bella means beautiful. And she is. Not just on the outside like girls in magazines or anything. She is a beautiful person. It takes a lot to make Bella angry, but when she is, you just need to get out of the way.

You know the girl who isn't super pretty or super smart or super anything, but there's something about her, some special thing, that makes people stop and smile when they see her? That's Bella. She has a gazillion friends and they're real friends, not just people filling up her cell phone list.

Ever since Dad left, Bella has been our family's glue. Mom tries hard, but there are days when I'm not sure that she's really with us. She's acting like everything's normal but I'm not fooled.

Bella is blonde and thin as a zipper, just like Mom. I definitely got Dad's genes. Bella always complains that I have olive skin and she missed out. I always thought that Bella was Mom's clone and I was Dad's. But lately, I'm not so sure.

Maybe I'm a whole lot more like Mom than I thought.

All I know is, thank God for Bella.

Not that I'd ever tell her that.

There are just some things you don't need to say.

14.

At the mall I find myself face-to-face with Angelique in Delia's. Though, actually, it is more face-to-fitting-room-door.

I am hovering outside Desi's door while she tries on a million different things, when Angelique's hand snakes over the top of a nearby cubicle door. She's holding something blue. I know it's her hand because she is wearing Eric's ring. It's a chunky Gothic thing but Angelique makes it look elegant.

"Could I have this in the pink, please?" she asks.

I look around. There isn't a sales assistant in sight.

"Sure," I say.

It's not as if I've got something better to do.

I head for the racks and dodge the helpful sales assistant.

Please understand that when I say "helpful," I am being sarcastic.

I finally spot a pink version of the frothy blue top I am holding when the assistant looms over from behind a rack of coats to make a suggestion.

"That's a lovely top," she says.

I nod and sidestep her, but she blocks my way.

"That's a size 4," she says, looking at me meaningfully.

"Uh-huh," I say.

"These tend to run small," she says. Then she pointedly looks me up and down and pulls out a size 10.

Sounds of the shopping mall fall away: the crash of carts, the kids crying, and the never-ending announcements of this hour's special. The sales assistant is smiling but looks smug, like she's bagged herself a trophy.

There are plenty of things I can think of to say to her. Like, do you realize you have lipstick on your teeth? Did you know that outfit you're wearing is meant for teenagers? Do they have a name for that hairstyle? Just thinking of these things makes me smile back at her.

"It's okay. It's not for me." I brush past her and return to the fitting rooms. "Here you go," I say, waving it over the top of Angelique's door.

"Thanks a lot," she says. The next moment

she bursts through her door to check it out in the full-length mirror against the back wall. She turns around a few times to get a look at the total effect. A little frown creases her perfect brow. "Hmmm."

"It looks good," I offer, even though these words nearly stick in my throat.

Angelique looks at me for the first time, registering that I'm not a sales assistant.

"Oh, hi!" she says.

She's realized I'm someone on her social fringe. She doesn't know my name. Then again, why should she? I wonder where all her friends are. Angelique usually has at least one or two fans wherever she goes. Maybe it is their day off.

"El, can you take some of this stuff?" complains Desi.

Half the store appears over her door. It takes me ages to put everything back on the hangers. During this time, Angelique stands in front of the mirror. Then she disappears into her fitting room and reappears in the blue top version. Finally she catches my eye in the mirror just as I glance at her.

"I hate shopping by myself," she says.

"Which top do you like the best?" I ask.

"I like the blue best," she says. "But Eric says pink is my color."

"So buy the top that you want to wear," I say. "I mean . . . you look good in anything."

Angelique gives me a nervous smile before disappearing back into her cubicle.

Desi finally decides on a cream silk tank top that she can't live without. Not surprisingly, it looks very similar to five other cream tops she has. As the cashier wraps the tank top, Angelique puts the blue top on the counter and takes out her wallet to pay for it.

"Thanks for your help," she says.

Desi squeezes my arm as we leave the shop and whispers incredibly loudly into my ear, "Omigod, that was Angelique Mendez."

"I know."

"I didn't know she knew you."

"She doesn't," I say.

Part of me is celebrating a victory for girls everywhere who dress for someone else. Another part is pleased that Eric will miss out on seeing his girlfriend dressed the way he wants.

Which is when I decide that I really am a horrible person. That I don't deserve anything good to happen to me. And even if Eric Callahan threw himself at my feet right now, I would just have to walk away. I would give him one long embrace, and say, "No really, please go back to Angelique. You deserve someone better than me."

Then I turn on my heel and bump into someone outside the store.

"Sorry," I say.

"Hey," Eric says, gripping my arm gently to steady me. "Are you okay?"

I swear violins begin playing right at that moment. The shopping mall lights glint off Eric's blond hair like we're in a shampoo commercial. I catch sight of his perfect teeth as his lips pull back in a slight smile. His breath is warm and minty in my face. I know I should be breathing but I've forgotten how. A puzzled look crosses his face, but is gone in an instant. Then he gives a little wave, so I wave back—until I realize he is waving to someone behind me. It is Angelique.

Eric lets go of my arm and I nearly fall to the floor. I realize the violins are just the Muzak wafting through the mall's speakers. I finally take a gulp of air.

"See ya," I say lamely, but he doesn't hear me.

"Omigod, that was Eric Callahan," says Desi.

I'd forgotten she was there.

"Wait until I tell Margot that you touched Eric Callahan in the mall."

"How about something to drink?" I say. "I've got some coupons."

"Can we share a large mocha? I love the mocha," says Desi.

If there's one thing I love about Desi, it's that she is easily distracted.

It's much later, after I lose Desi in the bathrooms, that I go back to Delia's and buy myself the pink top. I take the size 10. I don't try it on. I pay for it as if I'm making a drug deal, looking over my shoulder every three seconds like I'm about to be arrested, then I push it to the bottom of my bag. And it's like I'm two people in one body. There's the weird-acting me, who's just bought a pink frothy top that she actually doesn't like, and there's the other me watching the weird-acting me, thinking, "Hello, what's going on here?"

The two me's only get together when Desi tells me a joke as she leaves me at my front door. I feel a jolt as I snap back to reality and wonder how on earth I made it home.

15.

My Friday starts well, with an Eric sighting across the courtyard. He is bouncing a basketball, first with one hand then the other, through the gap between his walking legs. Just the sight of his broad shoulders and big hands makes me stop and watch until he's out of sight.

It's the second day of detention—make that my last day. I have thought of something to write. Desi and I get there early. There's a lanky-looking guy already sitting down. His legs barely fit under the desk.

"Basketball player," whispers Desi. "His name's Coop."

I already know this. He's one of the guys in the newspaper group.

I sit quietly, ignoring Dylan, who has come in and chosen to sit right next to me even though the room is full of empty desks, and I steadily fill the white space on the blue-lined paper. I use lots of dialogue, because this comes easily. I write about my first day of school. How Mom gave me my special schoolbag, with the pink lunch box and matching pink thermos, and kissed me quickly on the cheek. "Remember your manners, listen to your teacher, and don't chase boys," she'd said.

I write about the smells and the sounds and the strangeness of it all. About the boy who pulled at my hair ribbons. About the girl who became my best friend in five minutes. About the teacher who smelled like some flower that grew in my garden and who reminded me of home so that I cried and had to use her lace handkerchief. About Bella meeting me at lunch break and showing me off to all her friends. "This is my sister," she'd said. "Don't mind her, she's weird."

There are still five minutes of detention left when I finish counting my words. There are 494. I come up with a heading that takes me over the 500 mark—The First Day of the Rest of My Life. I count again—503.

I glance over at Dylan's page. He seems to be creating some artwork that has its origins at the gates of hell, with skulls and flames and spiderwebs. Nice. Desi has been fidgeting the entire time. She doesn't seem to have written much.

I stroll up to Ms. Clooney's desk and patiently wait for her attention. The red second hand on the large wall clock spins smoothly around the dial.

Well, don't mind me.

Whenever you're ready.

Finally Ms. Clooney looks up.

"Yes?" she asks.

"I've finished."

I wait while she reads. She is still reading when the end-of-lunch bell sounds.

"Right," she says finally.

I feel my shoulders drop a little as I relax.

"There's only one problem," she says, gathering her work together.

I hear Dylan shift in his seat.

"What?"

"There aren't five hundred words here," she says, handing me back the paper.

That's when I realize she hasn't been reading at all. She's been counting the words.

"There are five hundred three words," I say lamely. "I counted twice."

"Then you must have counted the title," she says. "The title doesn't count."

I grab a pen to write some extra words, but she is sailing out the door.

"See you Monday," she says.

I throw the pen at the door as she heads up the hall.

Desi picks it up and hands it back to me. "She really hates you."

Dylan shakes his head a little.

"Nah," he says. "As special as Ariel Ariel is, I think Clooney is just mean to everyone."

He hands me his artwork and turns to go.

He's out of uniform. I watch him walk out, his skinny-leg jeans clinging to his . . . clinging? Argh! I am losing it. I fix Eric in my mind.

"Pleasant thoughts," I whisper. "Pleasant thoughts."

But somehow Eric turns into Dylan, and Dylan's jeans are on an endless replay loop in my brain.

It's only later that night that I discover Dylan's artwork. I'd shoved it into my bag. Instead of the dragons and flames and the weird-looking plant that I'd seen before, it was a new piece. It was just patterns, curling into each other with lines and circles, all done in blue pen. Among the circles is a long number that I assume is his cell phone number.

As if!

16.

I add another thing to my list for Leonard. What does it mean, Leonard, I would ask, if a boy, a boy you don't like, gives you something—say a piece of paper with his cell phone number on it— and instead of shoving it into the garbage you hide it in your underwear drawer?

That'd stump him.

17.

Friday is movie night with Margot and Desi. It has been ever since I moved to Blair. But tonight I don't feel like leaving my cramped bedroom. This is the fifth day since I found out about Eric and Angelique, but the pain is still raw. I want to keep poking at it, just to make sure the wound is real. I need to do this in my own space. I want to wallow. When Bella yells out that Margot is at the door, I consider hiding under my comforter. Instead, my feet walk out of my room, I give Mom a peck on the cheek, and close the door quietly behind me, just in case the cat lady from next door pokes her head out her door as I leave. She is always doing this.

Cat Lady started talking to me a couple of months after we moved in.

"Nice weather for ducks," she said last week when it was raining.

I doubted even the ducks would be interested in standing in the rain. It was hitting the entry hall window at a 45-degree angle and threatening to break the glass.

Yesterday I caught her throwing tree branches over the fence.

"What's good for the goose is good for the gander," she'd said.

I started to think the woman was obsessed with poultry, so I just smiled politely.

"They dropped their stuff over here yesterday," she explained. "So how's your mom?"

She must have supersonic hearing. As soon as my door clicks shut she bustles outside with a watering can.

"Going out, dear?" she says, pretending to be surprised to see me.

"Yes," I say.

"Stay safe."

Actually, I'm just about to get abducted. I am just about to go on a drug-crazed rampage in a nearby abandoned warehouse. I am just about to steal lots of money so I can buy my family a new house and get the hell out of here. To get away from you.

Of course, I don't say this.

I grunt something to be polite then get into the car with Margot. Her sister, Steph, is driving us tonight and she says hi as I grapple with the tight seat belt in the back. It's only after I look up to see Margot staring at me that I realize I have missed something.

"Excuse me?" I ask.

"For the third time," says Margot with exaggerated patience, "what do you feel like seeing tonight?"

I shrug. I haven't even checked out the options in the paper.

We pick up Desi, who makes enough noise for the rest of us combined. She is wearing her new cream tank top, even though the chill air has me wearing a scarf.

"Nice top," says Margot, with a lift of her eyebrow. I don't know if she is being sarcastic or just her normal bored self.

Desi recounts our shopping expedition with a step-by-step description of my encounter with Eric. I'm sure she's already discussed it with Margot, but Margot acts like this is the first time she's heard about it.

"You didn't mention this to me," she says, her eyes narrowing.

I ignore her and look out the car window.

Margot continues to stare at me, but Desi is on a roll and talks all the way to the theater. When we get there, I thank Steph for the lift. The other two join me in the line as we gaze up at the flashing movie board.

"*Hearts Are*," reads Desi.

"No," Margot and I snap.

"*The Hidden Room, Black Water, Angelcake*—"

"*Angelcake*! That's a documentary," says Margot. "It's been nominated—"

"No," says Desi as I shake my head.

"*The Makeup Artist, Surfacing* . . ."

In the end we see *Black Water*. It's a thriller with a nice twist at the end that I never saw coming.

"Omigod, did you hear me scream when that guy popped up out of the water?" said Desi. "I mean, I thought it was the end, but then—"

"That device is so overdone." Margot yawns. "It was obvious from the start who the killer was."

Sometimes I wonder what it is like to be Margot. When I first met her she'd seemed so exotic, so different from anyone else I knew. And she'd made me laugh. But lately . . . Margot catches me staring at her and raises an eyebrow in query.

Desi is still gushing about the movie, when I excuse myself and slip into the bathrooms just to get some breathing space. A couple of people are staring into the large mirror above the sinks, applying makeup or fussing with their hair. I squirt some liquid soap into my palm and start washing my hands.

"Oh, hi!"

I look to my right to see Angelique. She's wearing her new blue top. She must have noticed me looking at it, because she picks at the fabric and says, "Eric likes it. I'm glad I chose the blue."

I murmur something but wonder if she is happy she chose the blue top because she loves it or because Eric does.

"I'm Angelique," she says, like it's some incredible revelation.

"I know," is all I say.

Then one of her friends joins her at the sink. As I slip away Angelique calls after me, "See ya."

But I just keep going.

In the lobby, Desi is still talking and Margot is checking out the movie posters on the wall.

"Are we going to eat?" says Margot, interrupting Desi.

We make our way upstairs to the food court. I order my budget hot chocolate, Desi has ice cream, and Margot has a bowl of french fries, coffee, and a slice of mud cake. Between mouthfuls, Margot points out the inconsistencies with the movie's plotline, the lead actor's lack of talent, and the uninspiring music, which belonged more in a Disney movie than a suspense film.

I'm only half listening to her.

Two tables away is a group from school. This is the jock group—the ones who play sports on Friday nights. They must have had an early game.

In the center of the group, Angelique is laughing and leaning into Eric's shoulder. He has that expression he often wears—the one that makes him look like he doesn't know what's going on.

And then I get a prickling feeling on the back of my neck. I look around and finally locate the source. Dylan is staring at me from the snack bar. He has seen me watching the golden couple and he gives me a little salute. This is the second time he's caught me watching Eric. I give Dylan my non-committal stare, but I'm feeling a little sick at being caught. His artwork still sits like a dirty secret in my underwear drawer at home.

Desi grabs my arm and gives me a little shake.

"Are you okay?" she asks. "You look weird."

Margot tilts her head back as Dylan approaches. He's swapped the jeans he was wearing at school for a newer-looking pair. He doesn't so much stop at our table as slide slowly past.

I sense Desi go into flirt mode as she sits up

straighter in her seat and pushes her hair away from her neck.

"Hello, Ariel Ariel," he says.

Then he disappears into the movie theater.

"Who was that?" demands Margot.

"Hmmm?" I'm carefully using my index finger to wipe out the hot chocolate froth in the bottom of my cup.

"That guy. That gorgeous guy."

"He's not gorgeous," I snap.

"He's in detention with El and me. And he's in our geography class. His name's Dylan. Dylan Shepherd," says Desi.

"So what's his story?" asks Margot.

"Story? I don't really know him. Hey, does anyone else want another drink?" I ask.

"And now El and Dylan have to work together for the geography field trip project."

"And Sarah," I add quickly.

"I think he's interested in El—," says Desi.

"Don't be ridiculous. Just because he wasn't interested in you, doesn't mean he's interested in me."

"Ouch! That's a bit low, El," says Margot.

"Well I think he's hot," says Desi, tapping her fingernails on the tabletop.

"If he's so hot, what's he doing going to the movies by himself?" I demand.

"Maybe he's meeting someone inside?" says Margot.

"Psh." The thought of someone waiting for Dylan, the thought of someone sitting next to Dylan in the dark, possibly holding his hand, makes me want to laugh wildly. In fact, I feel quite hysterical.

"You're so grouchy lately, El. You're just going to have to get over the fact that Eric isn't your property anymore. In fact, he never was," says Margot.

Eric? I thought we were talking about Dylan.

I try to stand up but I'm stuck on the bench seat behind the table.

"This has nothing to do with . . . you know who. You're both ridiculous, getting excited about some dropout from another school who just happens to look good in jeans—"

Margot gives me a look that says I'm making a fool of myself.

"Is he a dropout?" she asks with an interested gleam in her eye.

Trust her to pick on something I made up.

"I never mentioned his jeans," says Desi.

I pick up my bag.

"Did I mention his jeans?" repeats Desi.

"Drop dead," I say to no one in particular as I finally get out from behind the table.

"Now, what movie does this remind you of?" I hear Margot ask Desi as I stumble down the food court stairs.

18.

Mom picks us up. On the drive home, Desi and Margot act like nothing has happened, but I spend my time in the front seat feeling stupid and annoyed.

Sometime during the night—make that early morning—my sister, Bella, stumbles into our room and falls into bed. She smells like grease and french fries from her job at the fried chicken place. Sometime later she starts to snore softly. By then I'm awake and thinking about the mess that is currently my life.

The sight of Dylan catching me watching Eric and Angelique is on an endless loop in my brain. I finally get up and push my sister onto her side to stop her snoring.

"Night night," she mumbles.

I shove my feet into my fluffy slippers and go to the kitchen. In the fridge I find milk, moldy cheese, leftover green things, leftover brown things, and a chocolate bar wrapper—no chocolate. I tip the carton to my lips and let the cold milk trickle down my throat. The pink glow of the streetlight filters through the slats of the vertical blinds that are slightly open. It throws a barred pattern onto the spice rack wall.

The spice rack looks so huge here, yet it was just another kitchen thing in our Big, Big House. All the spices are in alphabetical order. I know this without looking. Just as I know that the books in Mom's bedroom are in order by author. Her wardrobe is color-coded—blue clothes together, pinks, whites—but mostly there are dull grays and browns. These are the things she can control. She used to have a little cupboard just for her shoes, but she's thrown out or given away most of them now. "Where would I wear them?" she answered when I asked why one day.

Mom spends her days making life better for "people in our community." That's how she describes her job. Sometimes I just wish she would spend time making our little community happier. I guess looking after Bella and me doesn't pay the bills. It's all about money. Mom likes to shop late at night to get the specials. I wonder if it's also so she doesn't meet up with anyone from our old life.

Outside, someone is kicking the mailboxes while they sing something that might be a song if it were in tune. The fridge motor starts up and joins in.

I sit on the counter and swing my legs, like I used to in our old house. The big house. The one with the Jacuzzi and the TV room. When we moved here, Mom said we were Downsizing. We'd gone from Big, Big House to Big House to apartment in three years.

You might think I'd hate living in a small apartment. But it's not all bad. We aren't going to be here long. Mom says this is a Minor Setback. I like that I can leave my bedroom door open and hear Mom breathing in her sleep in the next room. If I needed to get to her in the middle of the night it would only take ten big steps.

Not that I would.

I don't like living so close to other people, though. People I don't know. Don't even want to know. Cat Lady next door is always trying to talk to me. The guy upstairs sings in the shower before the sun is even thinking of coming up. Sometimes there's shouting, people racing up and down the stairs, people banging on doors late at night. I'm not used to so much noise.

Sometimes I wake at night and wonder where I am. The angles of the room are different. The ceiling is lower. There is a slight smell of mold underlying the smell of new carpet. Sometimes I wake to hear someone breathing near me and my heart races as I consider the possibilities. An intruder? A wild animal? Then I remember where I am. Sharing a room with Bella. Bella, who seems to have poured into this new life like liquid pours into a container. She has taken the shape of it without question.

Mom said we could paint our bedroom to brighten it up, but I wasn't really interested. It's just a room. We're not going to be here for that long.

Most of the kids at school have divorced parents, or mixed families, or single mothers, single fathers, so my fractured life is no big deal to everyone else. But it's a big deal to me. It's a nightmare that started almost two years ago when Dad walked out the door one day.

My best friend in elementary school was Sasha. In first grade I heard a teacher say that Sasha came from a broken home. And I felt so sad. I could just see her home, broken in two. The word "broken"—how weird. Like someone was careless. I guess people are.

I haven't talked to Dad since he left. Not much, anyway. The last time I did I said that I hated him, hated that he was the reason I had to move out of my home. Hated that since he'd left I'd lost the mother I used to know. That she'd been replaced by someone whose tired eyes creased at the edges like a crumpled envelope.

We never hug anymore.

The mailbox kicker is closer now. The song has changed to something less cheerful.

I ease myself slowly off the counter, put the milk in the fridge, and creep back to bed.

I listen for Mom's steady breathing down the hallway.

I wonder how I ended up in this life.

19.

The good thing about Fridays is that the next two days are days without school. No detention. No Ms. Clooney. No stupid rules.

The bad thing about Fridays is that the next two days are days without school. Days without Eric.

My life is an out-of-date gift card.

20.

At Monday detention I hand my essay to Ms. Clooney. I've made sure it's 520 words, just to be safe. She doesn't even look at the pages and I'm free to go. As I leave Dylan and Desi behind, I can feel Dylan's eyes boring into my back.

It only takes Desi one more day to get out of detention. It only takes me two whole days to get back into trouble.

Margot and I are waiting in the cafeteria line on Wednesday when someone pushes in front of a seventh-grade kid. This is normal and I would have let it go, but the little kid doesn't understand the rules. Maybe he's a bit slow or something. He tries to push his way forward again and gets a knock on the head for his troubles. I'm standing right behind him and he falls back onto me, totally humiliated.

"Hey, careful," I say to the guy who pushed in front.

He's as tall as a house and he's sporting long, fuzzy sideburns.

While I'm checking out his sideburns, he shoves his face into mine, and then pushes me.

Margot is hanging on to my arm.

"Forget it," she says. "Let's go."

I shake her off and shove him back. I'm not sure who's more surprised—him or me. But suddenly I can't take it anymore. It's like a sleeping monster has awakened in the pit of my stomach. Adrenaline rushes through my arms, sings in my ears. I'm sick of dodging and weaving and keeping out of trouble's way. I want to take it on.

I want someone to pay.

As I raise my hand again, a teacher shows up and tells us both to go to the office.

Ms. Clooney finds me, alone, outside the staff room. The bully wasn't so dumb after all, and he's escaped to push another day. Ms. Clooney doesn't ask me why I'm there. For once, she seems pleased to see me. She loads me up with a pile of colored paper sheets and leads me to the announcement booth.

The announcement booth is just a little room with a table, a chair, some shelves, a bench, a board with switches, a microphone, and a little window that looks out onto the main hall. It's a place that I'd mostly ignored until now.

"Our Wednesday announcer has left," she explains. "We're running a little late. Just get through what you can."

She shoves me down into a swivel seat behind a microphone. She says something about switches and pink forms and blue forms and school stamps for authenticity. Then she leaves the booth in a whirl of efficiency and I'm left with a pair of headphones in my hands.

The adrenaline rush from the cafeteria encounter has gone, and I'm left feeling slightly sick.

A sheet of paper on the bulletin board in front of me says "Welcome to SRN—Student Radio News." Someone has added "where no news is good news."

The vice principal comes in.

"You're late," she says, before flicking a switch.

I don't bother to tell her I'm not the regular Wednesday announcer. I guess we all look the same in our school uniform. But then, how hard can it be? I lean in to the microphone.

"Umm, good afternoon, everyone. This is Radio—"

The vice principal sticks her head in and hisses,

"There's no need to yell—that's what the microphone is for."

"Radio SRN," I continue, a little quieter. "And today's notices are . . ."

I read through a list of notices that have been duly authorized by the official school stamp. I announce missing textbooks, blazers, and sports uniforms. I advise that the auditions for the school play will be held next week; that the chocolate drive chocolates and money are due back the next day; that someone called Suzy loves someone called Muffy. (Too late, I realize that last page did not sport the official school stamp.) I move on to the upcoming dance and calls for volunteers.

All in all I do a pretty good job. I can't resist inserting my own notice into the mix. The notice that says people caught pushing in the cafeteria line will be put on yard duty for a week.

Then the bell rings. I flick a switch and poke my head out of the booth looking for a quick getaway. Ms. Clooney appears from nowhere.

"You've got Wednesdays," is all she says.

21.

"Just tell her you can't do it," whispers Margot from behind her science textbook. "Get a note from your mom. Tell her you get claustrophobic."

"She can't make you miss out on lunch. It's a student's right," says Desi.

Margot and Desi are devastated. I will now not be available for Wednesday lunch library sessions. I'm not sure how I feel. I want to ask them if they heard me. How I sounded.

Meg Piper slips me a note about the next student council meeting. Something about extra court time for the girl's basketball team during the next month. I check my day planner and realize that there is a council meeting the next day.

"Just tell her," says Desi.

I find myself agreeing that I'll get out of Radio SRN somehow.

22.

Wednesday is Leonard's day. I go there straight after school, hang around a bit, then go home. On Wednesdays Mom works late, so Bella and I usually have something like noodles or eggs for dinner. I'm thinking whether I will have eggs or noodles, or maybe both, when I cruise into Leonard's office.

When I get to Leonard's I usually go straight into his office, which is upstairs. This day, however, the door's closed, so I sit in the waiting room and check out the posters on the walls. There's a cute kitten clinging to a tree branch. "Hang in there" it says underneath.

Hmmm.

On another poster there is a chimpanzee that looks remarkably like Leonard. I wonder if it is one of his children.

The door to Leonard's office opens and a woman and child look my way then scuttle downstairs.

Leonard ushers me inside and I take a seat and notice an umbrella leaning up against it.

"Damn," says Leonard. "I'll just be a minute."

He grabs the umbrella and hurries downstairs.

Leonard's office is neat. He has a desk with a family photo, a phone, a jar of pens, and an unused writing pad. Over near the window is where we sit—on old leather armchairs that look like he picked them up in a secondhand shop. There's another armchair, unmatching, against the wall. We sit opposite each other like we're friends about to have a chat. To the side of our chairs is a coffee table with a box of tissues on it, and a clock that faces Leonard. There is a garbage can next to me for the tissues—for all the crying I'm not doing when I don't talk to Leonard.

In the corner of the room is a large box of toys and a two-story doll's house. The house even has a garage with a cute pink car inside. There's paper and crayons and even a toy gun. Now I knew what Leonard did in his spare time.

"The toys are for my younger clients," he says, appearing out of nowhere, a little out of breath.

I raise my eyebrows—as if I cared.

Leonard looks a little hassled today. Usually he makes me feel like I should clean my shoes. But today his hair—what's left of it—is standing up like he's run his fingers through it. His shirt is looking twisted and untidy.

He tidies the toys. By the time he sits opposite me he has used up ten minutes of my time, which is great. He is still holding on to the pink car from the doll's house and absentmindedly rolling the car wheels over his palm.

"How are you, Ariel?" he asks.

I ignore him and look out the window. A drizzle of rain makes things smudgy, like a watercolor painting that hasn't yet dried. The last of the trees' brown leaves are turning mushy. I try not to think of anything, just in case he can read my mind. We sit like this for some time, until Leonard feels the need to talk. He always has to spoil things. I try to ignore him but something he says ricochets off the back of my skull.

"I know it's hard for you . . . ," he says. His lips are turned down in an expression of grief.

"I beg your pardon?" I say in my best Margot voice.

Leonard looks pleased. I have broken my silence again. Something to report back to my mother.

". . . hard for you—," he repeats.

I cut him off midsentence.

"Leonard, you don't know me. Just 'cause my mom tells you stuff, you think you know me? Well, you don't. You don't know what it feels like to be me."

Leonard loses his undertaker's down-turned lips. He replaces it with a blank face.

I bet your kids play violin and speak five languages and never have to tidy their bedrooms because you have a cleaning lady.

Am I right, Leonard?

I bet your wife plays tennis and drives a sports car and has her own personal hairdresser.

I bet she feels bad about the poor people and always makes a donation when the Salvation Army volunteers ring their bells at the traffic lights, because it makes her feel better.

I bet you're thinking about getting a personal trainer now that you're not getting younger or— let's face it, Leonard—skinnier.

I bet you have a new Mercedes and you pay someone else to wash it.

I bet you've wondered if those hair replacement centers could do something about your balding head.

I bet the closest you get to feeling sad is when your football team loses.

Of course, I don't say any of these things.

My volcano of anger suddenly stops erupting. In its place is nothing and it's pure and clean and right. I push myself out of the chair and lean closer.

Leonard's eyes widen slightly, like he thinks maybe I'm going to hit him. He reminds me of the cafeteria sideburns guy and for a moment I'm tempted to. Instead I grab the pink car from him, set it on the windowsill, and give it a big push. I hear it fall onto the polished floorboards as I make my way to the door with forty-five minutes of my session still left to go.

23.

Sometime later that night I call Leonard's answering machine. I wait for his recorded message to finish and then listen to the silence waiting for me to fill it up.

24.

It's the last Thursday of the month, which means student council meeting time. A wasted lunchtime. In the morning I have geography and Mr. Ray reminds everyone to bring back their parent approval forms for next Tuesday's field trip. I'm too busy thinking about the student council meeting and wishing it was over.

I am our class rep for student council because of bad timing. On the day of the election I was home with a bad case of hating-schoolitis. When I complained to Bella later, she told me that that's what I got for staying home from school. Now that she's at college, she's obviously forgotten that you need days off from school sometimes. Desi said that it wasn't fair because I didn't have a chance to reject the nomination, but our homeroom teacher, Ms. Diamond, dismissed that idea outright. All she wanted was to check the class rep election off her to-do list.

The position of class rep is usually reserved for the most serious or boring or loudest student in class.

So what does that make me?

Most of the time it's just me and Desi and Margot hanging out, but for the couple of days a month before the meeting I become the most sought-after girl in my class.

"Tell them about the heating," says Henry. This is always his problem. Henry Loudner has a constant runny nose and wears a scarf every day— even in summer. "It needs turning up. They'll pay for the bills if I end up with pneumonia."

He pronounces pneumonia with a "p," but I don't correct him. He has never taken a sick day in his life.

"Can you mention the cafeteria prices?" asks Jess. "I mean, the cafeteria is supposed to be a student service, isn't it? Not some rip-off joint."

"We need more access to the gym," says Emmett.

I want to say to them, "You've got a voice. You tell them."

But I'm their voice at student council. So I turn up once a month to Room 124D and battle for them—each and every ungrateful one of them.

Sometimes what they want is so ridiculous I wonder if they're joking.

Like the time Desi wanted hair dryers in the girls' bathrooms. Hair dryers! Like it's some beauty salon or something. Or the time Chris asked for healthy food to be served at the cafeteria.

I mean, are these people kidding or what?

Whatever they ask for, I take their messages and sit around one lunchtime a month and argue that it's a perfectly reasonable request to have a hair dryer in the girls' bathroom and argue and argue until we come to an agreement that maybe a request for hair dryers in just the locker rooms in the gym would be okay. Or that something should be done about the rip-off prices at the cafeteria that only sells crap.

And most times I get somewhere. Which is just as well, because if I didn't I would keep arguing until everyone else around the council table got so sick of me that they would agree to anything just to shut me up.

Margot says that maybe I could get a job as an ambassador at the United Nations one day. She got Desi to look it up in the career guide in the library, and Desi came back to tell us it wasn't listed. She's so naive sometimes but that's what I love about her.

Anyway, it's the last Thursday of the month and I'm heading to the meeting when I see Eric coming my way up the hall. His hair is doing that flopping-into-his-face kind of thing and I want to reach up and smooth it away when something incredible happens. He stops right in front of me.

"Hey," he says.

I turn to look behind me, but there's no one else around.

"El?" he asks.

I look back at him and nod, unable to speak.

"You're in Meg Piper's class, right?"

I nod again. Eric leans against the wall next to my head. This means I have to look up at him a little less. If I stood on tiptoe I could plant a kiss on his perfect lips. I can feel the heat coming off his body in waves and his Eric smell, which is a mixture of mothballs, just-baked bread, and peppermint gum.

"You're Meg's class rep for student council?"

"Yep." I figure I have to say something. It's the best I can do.

Eric is looking serious and I'm wondering what the problem is. Perhaps he wants to solve world poverty. Or discuss the finer points of Math 2. Maybe Meg's in trouble?

While my mind has been conjuring possibilities,

Eric has been talking. I finally tune in to hear, ". . . can see our problem. I mean, I'm all for girls' sports, but the next game is really important for us."

"Finals?" I repeat.

"The basketball finals," he says earnestly, sweeping hair out of his eyes.

"And you want me to . . ."

"I know Meg's asking for equal practice time on the court. It's just that the boys need it more. We're prepared to give them two after-school nights and we'll take three. Not Fridays, because that's when we play. That's reasonable, don't you think?"

I find myself agreeing with him that it's perfectly reasonable and he leans in and squeezes my shoulder.

"I knew you'd be okay with this. Dylan said—"

"Dylan?"

Suddenly Eric looks troubled and he squeezes my shoulder again. It's hot where he's touching me and I don't want him to stop.

"He thought you wouldn't go for it. So we're all good?" he asks.

I agree. We're all good.

And later, when I'm asked at student council whether I have any business this month, I say, "No, we're all good."

25.

After lunch, when Meg asks me how student council went, I shake my head.

"Crap! Maybe we can find some court time somewhere else," she says.

"Maybe I could go to the principal," I suggest lamely. "I mean, there's probably an equal opportunity issue here."

Meg shakes her head. "Don't worry. I know you tried your best. Thanks anyway."

And that's when I get mad. And strangely, the person I'm angry with isn't Eric. Dylan said? Who did he think he was? He'd only known me for two minutes and . . . why was he talking to Eric about me? The thought of Dylan's eyes on me as I drooled over Eric made my heart thud in my chest.

Dylan had to be stopped before he got completely out of control.

26.

At the end of the day, I hang around the lockers and try to work out which is Dylan's. After fifteen minutes the hallway is practically empty and no Dylan has emerged. It's only later that I wonder if I should have checked the coffin room.

At home I uncover the hidden treasure that is Dylan's artwork and lock myself in the bathroom with my cell phone. I punch in Dylan's number carefully from the page and wait. The phone rings and then Dylan's voice cuts in.

"Hello?" he says.

"Dylan, it's Ariel. El Marini."

But it's just his voice mail.

"Ah, yeah, you've called Dylan. Leave your name and number and I'll call you back."

I can't think of anything to say so I hang up and add Dylan's number to my contact list. Then Bella pounds on the door and asks me what the hell I'm doing, so I stuff the artwork and my phone under my sweater and flush the toilet. I spray the air freshener for effect.

When I emerge, she sniffs the air and asks if I was reading on the toilet.

I roll my eyes and push past her. "Don't be disgusting," I say.

"Margot called," she says, before slamming the bathroom door in my face.

But when I dial Margot's number, she's busy.

27.

The thought of Eric pitying me is more than I can bear. I have this scenario going on in my head where Dylan has a deep and meaningful talk with Eric about how I have the hots for him. For Eric, that is. The whole thing is making me sick.

I don't see either of them first thing Friday morning; though at one stage I think I see the back of Dylan's head. I grab his arm. He turns around and it's not Dylan at all.

I finally see Dylan at lunchtime. I am sitting in the library with Margot and Desi and we're talking. Rather, Margot is talking. She's doing a perfect imitation of Mr. Isolde, our English teacher, and I'm trying not to laugh too loud. Desi wipes tears from her eyes, while begging Margot to stop, but this just makes Margot exaggerate even more.

I volunteer to grab some tissues from the librarian's desk (hasn't Desi heard of waterproof mascara?) and when I'm there I notice Dylan outside the library window.

I drop a tissue into Desi's lap, mumble a lie about the bathroom, then disappear outside.

It takes me a couple of minutes to find Dylan. He's sitting alone on a seat in the shaded area and it looks like he's been waiting for me.

"Hello, Ariel Ariel," he says, shifting along the seat in invitation.

I sit down abruptly.

"My name's El," I say. "Why are you so annoying?"

Dylan shrugs but looks pleased, like I've paid him a compliment.

"What are you doing outside, Ariel? Don't you usually hang out in the library?"

"I need to talk to you," I say.

"So talk," says Dylan.

"It's about Eric," I begin.

Dylan looks at me blankly.

"Eric Callahan."

Dylan looks blank again.

"Eric Callahan," I repeat. "He's your friend, isn't he? You seemed to know each other in detention."

"So?" says Dylan. He looks a little annoyed now.

"So, what did you say to him?"

"About . . . ?"

"About me!" I say, annoyed that I have to say it aloud.

Dylan leans back, resting his arms across the top of the seat. "Why would I be saying anything?"

"Eric mentioned you'd been talking about me."

I lean back into the seat, then jerk forward again when I touch Dylan's arm.

Dylan frowns. "I don't think so," he says.

"Yes," I insist. "Extra time on the basketball court. Student council. You said I'd make a fuss."

Dylan shrugs. "Oh, that."

He says it like it's not worth discussing but there's something in his eyes that dismisses me as a loser.

"What?" I demand.

He shakes his head. "Nothing."

"What?"

"Eric just ran the idea past me. About asking you not to mention the extra court time for the girls' basketball team. I told him you'd never go for it."

"Oh." I stand up to leave. "Well, I guess you don't know everything," I say.

"Guess not," he says.

The way he says it makes me feel like I've been judged. As if I've let him and myself down.

28.

eonard. Leonard, Leonard, Leonard.

I'm so tired, Leonard. Some nights I just can't sleep. If you were around then, Leonard, we'd definitely have a nice little talk. But Wednesdays come and it's daytime and I don't need to talk to you then.

Mom thinks I have nightmares, Leonard, but I don't. It's worse than that. I have nice dreams. I dream that everything is back to normal. That my family is all together and back in our real home and life is good.

It's when I wake from these dreams, a smile still curling up my mouth, that the truth hurts. And that's when I cry, Leonard.

Margot says I'm a dreamer, but she's wrong.

I'm living in reality. It's just that I don't want to be here.

29.

On Friday afternoon I pretend to have a cold so I don't have to go to the movies with Margot and Desi. It's true, kind of. My nose is stuffy.

Margot and Desi sit together all day, which is fine by me. At lunchtime we still hang out in the library and I don't need to say much because Desi's doing all the talking. She's having one of her up days. Angelique swans by and says, "Hi!"

Desi stops midsentence and calls out loudly, "Hi, Angelique," as if she wants the whole world to know that Angelique has spoken to her. I grunt a reply but Margot just stares at me, her eyes trying to uncover my secrets.

I excuse myself and go to the bathroom. I spend the rest of lunchtime in the last stall on the left, sitting on the lid of the seat and reading the graffiti on the walls. I'm always interested to see the latest gossip.

When I get home from school, I set myself up to veg out on the couch. But Mom has other ideas.

"School shoes," she says, holding out one of my shoes like it's diseased.

It's true; my shoes have taken on a life of their own. The straps broke ages ago and I cut them off to avoid the flapping. The sole of one has lifted away from the top of the shoe and now gapes, smiling to the world whenever it takes a step. I'd never get away with it at my old school.

"They're comfortable," I complain.

But we are going to the mall for a quick shopping trip.

I hate shopping with Mom. The only way she shops is quick. I like to browse and check out what's on sale. Bella is working, so she misses out.

The trip starts badly. We are just walking through the main doors, when Mom spies one of my old school friends nearby.

"Oh, look," she says. "Isn't that Melanie? From Regis?"

It is Melanie—Mel Furlong, a girl I used to hang around with in my other life. I shake my head and try to drag Mom the other way. Of course, she has other ideas.

"Mel-an-ee," calls out Mom, waving to get her attention.

Could this woman be any more embarrassing?

I consider creeping away, but Mel is coming over. She looks nervous and I don't blame her.

"Hello," she says.

"Hi," I say, checking out the mall's floor pattern.

"I haven't seen you for ages," says Mel. "How is . . . how are things?"

I don't answer, so Mom kicks in and blabs on about our new life and really Melanie should come and visit one day and hasn't-it-been-ages and my-hasn't-Melanie-grown. Like Mel's some magical bean in a fairy story.

Finally Mom stops and Mel promises to drop by one day. Then she leaves and I realize that she hasn't bothered to find out our address and I know that there isn't a single moment that any of us have believed that she will visit. And it feels kind of sad that Mel, a girl I used to have sleepovers with, sat next to at school, and swapped lunches with is now just someone I used to know.

"You should contact Those Girls," says Mom, for what must be the thousandth time.

Mom doesn't understand I can't. It would be like having one foot in my old life and one foot in the new. I had to choose, and for now I'm hanging out with Margot and Desi. When I go back to Regis High School, things will change again.

Margot and Desi are always ready to put down Regis. I think of my life without them and my mind shuts down. It just doesn't want to go there.

At the shoe store, I'm sitting on a large over-stuffed seat—one sock on, one sock off—when someone bumps me from behind.

"Sorry."

I turn around to see Angelique. She is trying on an athletic shoe and giggles when the sales assistant arrives with a black leather shoe for me.

"School shoes," we say as one.

"You'd think they could come up with something that actually looks okay to wear," she says.

I shake my head. "I think that's against the law of school uniform design," I say. I hold up two different shoes. "So you choose between Chunky Prom Queen and Pretty Preschooler."

Angelique just shakes her head.

Mom's giving me that "determined to be introduced stare," but I'm ignoring her. Finally she says, "El, won't you introduce me to Your Friend?"

Now Angelique definitely knows my name. Somehow it was better when she didn't.

I introduce Mom to Angelique, who of course is very polite in return.

"You should drop by one day," I hear Mom say,

as I fumble with the buckle on my shoe. The blood is rushing in my ears loudly as Mom gives Angelique our address. A look that I don't understand flashes over Angelique's face.

"She's a Nice Girl," says Mom as Angelique leaves the store with a wave.

"I think this is the wrong size," I say loudly.

When I get home, I call Margot's cell phone. She picks up but can't hear me because there's too much noise in the background. She asks if I'm feeling better, then promises to call me over the weekend. There's laughter in the background and she says she's got to go. I hang up, wishing I'd never called.

30.

It's Saturday and Mom is grocery shopping. Bella has planned to visit Dad and asks me for the third time whether I'd like to tag along. I'm sitting in the room that is our kitchen and dining and living room all in one, watching Saturday morning kids' shows because I can. The couch I'm sitting on—way too big for this unit, but we can't afford a new one—is littered with used tissues, the plate that my toast was on, and remote controls, because I can never figure out which is which. My pretend cold has taken on a life of its own. I've stemmed the dripping of my nose by shoving a tissue up each nostril.

"No thanks," I say, though it sounds like, "Dough tanks."

Bella taps her foot like I'm letting her down. I don't know why she still bothers asking me. "Any message?" she asks finally.

I shake my head and turn up the volume.

A cartoon character has been sliced and diced then miraculously re-formed. I hear the door slam as Bella leaves. A minute later I've thought of a message for Dad so I drag myself off the couch, rush to the door, and poke my head outside. But Bella has gone. Instead I see Angelique slouching past.

"Angelique?" I say.

Her eyes meet mine for the briefest of split seconds, and then she is gone—disappearing up the side steps in a blur of red jacket. I go back inside and doze on the couch. When I wake, I wonder if I have dreamed the whole thing. This seems the most likely. That I have dreamed Angelique Mendez would be walking past my door in my grungy neighborhood on a Saturday morning when I have a temperature of a hundred gazillion.

31.

By the next afternoon my temperature is down to nearly normal. I have claimed the couch as mine, with pillows and my comforter, remote control, and tissues at hand. Bella is out with her friends and Mom is hanging wet clothes on a drying rack in front of the heater next to the TV.

"Can't you put them in the dryer?" I ask crossly.

"The dryer died," says Mom cheerfully. "This will save on the electricity bills."

"Great." I collapse back against the pillows.

"Can I get you anything before I go next door?"

"Next door?" I ask.

"Yes. Peggy needs a hand with her curtains."

"Peggy? Oh, Cat Lady."

"Peggy is a lovely lady. Show some respect," snaps Mom, and somehow I'm happier with an angry Mom than a sad one.

"Do we have any chicken noodle soup?" I ask.

"We have cream of tomato," says Mom.

I shake my head. Then she rattles off a whole list of things we have, none of which I want. I shake my head again.

"Don't worry," I say. "I'm not really hungry."

Then someone knocks on the door before she can get going on her favorite medical topic—feed a cold and starve a fever.

"That's probably Peggy now," says Mom.

Imagine her surprise when she opens the door to find Dylan standing there.

Imagine my surprise.

"Is Ariel in?" he asks.

Mom straightens slightly and whisks her chores apron off.

"Yes," she says. "Yes, she is. Come in. El!" she calls out as though I'm not just three steps away. Then she turns back to Dylan. "I'm sorry, you are . . . ?"

"Dylan. Dylan Shepherd. I go to school with Ariel. Nice to meet you, Mrs. Marini." Then he holds out his hand politely and I nearly die when they shake hands.

The sight of him has set up a niggle in the empty cavern that is my brain.

I am in my pajamas. The ones with the cute monkeys on them. The ones that say *Good Night,*

Sleep Tight. I pull the comforter over me and hope
he hasn't seen me.

"There's a Nice Young Man to see you, El,"
Mom calls out.

Nice Young Man? Maybe Dylan has brought
a friend with him. I peek out from under the
comforter.

Mom's making faces at me, moving her eyebrows
up and down, her lips a surprised pursed oval.

"I'm not really up for visitors," I say, but Mom
has already let Dylan through the door.

"Please, call me Isobelle," Mom insists.

Please, pass me the basin. Dylan Shepherd is in
my home. Black hoodie and all.

"Hello," I say, in a voice that clearly says What
the hell are you doing here?

Mom's making signs behind his back, which are
just annoying. The kind of signs that mean, "He's
a Nice Boy and where have you been hiding him?"
It's the happiest she's looked in ages, but I'm not in
the mood.

Dylan turns around and nearly catches her at
it. Mom asks if he would like a hot drink. He says
no, then sits down in the rocking chair as if he's
settling in.

"Well, I just need to go next door then," says

Mom loudly, as if we're all deaf. "Nice to meet you, Dylan. Feel free to drop in any time."

Then she disappears out the door before I have a chance to say anything. The door clicks shut loudly.

"Well," says Dylan.

"What are you doing here?"

"Geography project," he says.

The niggle says "Bingo." "Oh, right," I say aloud.

"Are you sick?" he says.

"No," I say, pulling the comforter up toward my chin. "I always lie around on Sundays in my pajamas."

"Oh," says Dylan, looking around.

"That was a joke," I explain, just in case he didn't get it.

"I thought it was sarcasm," he says lightly.

I think back to my first idea of Dylan. Bored. Macho. Thick. Suddenly I feel really warm and I wonder whether my fever's back.

"This is a nice place," he says.

"It's just temporary," I say. I don't know why I have to tell him this.

He shrugs and pulls out some paper from his back pocket. He unfolds it and thrusts it at me. It's our geography project info sheet.

"Where's that girl?" he asks.

"Sarah?"

"Yeah. The bossy one."

"I guess she'll be here any minute," I say.

Dylan looks like he's settled into the rocking chair for the duration. His jeans have crept up his legs while he's sitting and I notice that he is wearing two different socks. I wonder if maybe he can't afford a matching pair.

"So . . ."

The TV is blaring away and I stare at the screen without really seeing it.

We watch three ads, all of them loud, and none of them make any sense.

"So how long have you and Eric Callahan known each other?" I finally get the courage to ask.

"A while," he says.

There are plenty of things I would like to ask Dylan. Who is Eric's favorite band? What's his favorite movie? Do you think he'd go out with a girl like me?

"Did you find my place okay?" I ask.

"I've been here before. Angelique's brother lives here. Upstairs."

Shower man.

"Angelique's brother? How do you know Angelique?" I say.

Dylan waves his hand in the air impatiently as if he doesn't want to talk about it, then finally says, "Eric's my cousin."

"You're Eric Callahan's cousin?" I repeat.

Callahan. Shepherd.

"Our mothers are sisters," he says.

I get it, of course. It's just that I can't think of two guys less like each other than Eric and Dylan.

"Do you want a drink?" I need to move. My mind is crowded with the information. I just want to go somewhere quiet and work out what it means.

"Coffee would be good," he says even though five minutes before he didn't want a drink.

I wander into the kitchen, careful to keep the comforter covering me and turn the electric kettle on. I decide to make a dash for my bedroom to get changed and bump into Dylan who is standing right behind me. The comforter drops out of my hands and Dylan reaches down and gives it to me. He now has a perfect view of my little-kid pajamas.

"Going to change," I mumble.

I throw on some clothes from my bedroom floor, look in the mirror and decide against brushing my hair. I don't want to look like I'm trying.

Back in the kitchen I make him an instant coffee and hoist myself up onto my favorite spot on the counter. Dylan doesn't talk so I fill in the gaps. I ask questions and he answers using the least amount of words he can. I wonder if it's a game with him.

I find out that he lives two blocks away. He lives with his mother and father and his really little brother. His grandfather lives in an addition on the back of their house.

"What's it like living with your grandfather?" I ask, but he just shrugs.

"You know," he says.

"I don't," I say.

"Him and my dad don't get along so well," he says. "But I like having him around. He's pretty out there for an old guy. He has a mean sense of humor. I guess I used to hang out more with him when I was younger. He gave me my first paint set."

Dylan has just put more than two sentences together. I should be celebrating, but I can't stop thinking about Eric.

"Why don't they get along?" I ask.

He shrugs. "They're too different. Or maybe they're too much the same. I've never worked that out."

"How come you moved schools?" I ask.

"I felt like a change," he says, so sharply that I don't have the nerve to ask why.

"Are you good at math?" I ask.

"No," he says.

"Are you going to join the basketball team?" I ask. "Have you ever been to one of Eric's games?"

"No," Dylan says. "I don't like playing games."

Then I remember my good manners and ask if he wants a cookie.

"Thanks," he says.

"I'm sure Sarah will be here any minute," I say, looking pointedly at the kitchen clock. I can't remember what time we made our meeting.

Then I shove a box of cookies under Dylan's nose and watch him devour half of it, carefully pulling the cookie halves apart and licking the cream from the center, then dunking the rest of the cookie into his coffee. Watching him do this makes me feel unsettled.

"So, do you have any ideas about the project?" I ask. I'm not really interested. It's just that the kitchen has been shrinking and Dylan is invading my personal space. I have an urge to reach out and trace the white scar that runs from his lips. I sit on my hands.

Dylan shrugs. "Projects aren't really my thing."

"Really? It's just that Eric—"

"You've really got it bad for him, haven't you?" he says quietly.

"What?"

"I saw you in detention. You have the hots for him," says Dylan casually. "But he already has a girlfriend—remember? So maybe you should, like, back off."

"What?" I repeat. My body is still and I've forgotten how to breathe. Tears sting the back of my eyeballs. I feel them escape and slide slowly down my cheeks. I don't make an idiot of myself by moaning or gasping or shrieking. All my noise is clogged in my throat, but the tears pour out like some efficient fire sprinkler.

Dylan grabs a paper towel and leans in close. He swipes at the tears on my cheeks then grabs my nose like I'm a little kid and says, "Blow."

So I blow and mumble that I have a cold.

Then Mom bursts in, on a quick excursion for more pins.

"Don't let me interrupt." She grabs her sewing box and disappears again without once looking at us.

Dylan moves away and the phone rings. I get down off the counter to answer it. It's Sarah. She's stuck at home with her little brothers, still waiting for her mom to return from a quick trip to the mall. She promises to make it as soon as she can.

"Don't bother," I say, trying to sound as normal as possible. "Let's catch up in class."

"I've gotta go," Dylan mumbles as I hang up. He's already worked out there's no geography project happening today.

Then he leaves and I stumble back to the couch and turn on the TV. I can't see the whole screen because the drying rack is covering it slightly.

That's when I realize that my washed underwear has been on display for the whole world to see.

32.

Our school uniform is red and black and white. It's compulsory, but everyone manages to make their own statement. Margot's going through a crimson phase, so she adds little accents, like her bird necklace, that she can quickly hide when it's inspection time.

The uniform colors are the only colors I wear, apart from my old pajamas. Everything else is black. I don't count the pink top in my drawer because I haven't worn it yet.

When I go to school I wear my uniform.

When I'm not at school I wear black.

I wear black because it is easy.

I wear black because it is cool.

It is cool like the black silence of a deep well.

Like the secret depths of a limestone cave.

Or the stillness of a long dark night.

And when I see someone else, someone wearing black, our eyes meet and we know. We know why black.

33.

By Monday I am well enough to go to school. How disappointing. I realize Margot didn't call me on the weekend. She apologizes and I tell her not to worry about it. She and Desi are full of news from last Friday night's movie. We are sitting in our usual spot on the carpeted floor of the biography section in the library. I have one ear on them and both eyes on the glassed-in meeting room where the newspaper group is in session. Even though everyone is sitting in a circle of chairs, it is easy to see who the leader is. I watch as Angelique prompts questions, makes notes, and directs the discussion. The room is mostly soundproof, so I am only guessing what is really going on. At one point she stares straight out at me, as if aware that I'm watching her. The stare reminds me of her appearance near my house last Saturday and then I'm positive that it was no dream.

I suddenly make the connection that she had probably been visiting her brother.

". . . fixed it?" asks Desi, tugging at my sleeve.

"Excuse me?"

"Your Wednesday radio gig. Is your mom going to complain?" asks Desi.

"Why don't you join them?" says Margot.

She has seen me watching the newspaper group.

"What?" I laugh as if I don't know what she's talking about.

"The newspaper nuts. Maybe you should discover what you're missing out on?" Her eyes are two slits of dark granite.

"I don't—," I say.

Desi cuts in. "Hey, that could be fun. Maybe we could all join. I'd love to know what they talk about in there."

"Who cares?" I say.

Margot has already unfolded herself from the floor. I watch her straighten her skirt, smooth her hair, and walk to the meeting room. Desi follows quickly behind.

I don't know what to do. At the last minute I race quickly after Desi before the meeting room door shuts behind her.

"Hello," says Angelique with a smile.

34.

"Did you see her nails?" repeats Desi for perhaps the fourteenth time.

"Yes," I answer, flipping to the back of my math textbook for an answer.

"I mean, they were professionally done. Professional. I should know, because my cousin Kiera works in a salon. Not that there's anything wrong with your nails, El."

Desi hasn't shut up since we invaded the newspaper group at lunchtime. She is fascinated with Angelique and acts like we've been in the presence of a movie star. She's also careful to let me know that I am her friend and she's on my side when it comes to the whole Eric saga.

Strangely, Margot has barely said anything. All she said as we got to our lockers was, "Well, that was interesting."

As usual, I can't decide whether she really meant it was interesting or if she was mocking it. I don't know what to make of the meeting. There seemed to be a lot of talk about what people were going to do, but so far no one seemed to be doing anything. Nobody except Angelique and the guy called Coop, the one from detention, who was writing an article on the school basketball team.

"I heard her father is some famous journalist," says Desi.

"Who?" I erase my math scribbles and start again.

"Angelique's dad. And her mom used to be a model. I've never heard of her, but she was big in Europe years ago. She lives in France."

"Who does?"

"Angelique's mother. If I was Angelique, I'd live in France. Imagine the clothes. Do you think she uses French products on her hair? Not that there's anything wrong with your hair, El."

Ms. Clooney cruises by like a shark on food patrol. She pauses long enough to rest her fingertips on Desi's textbook before moving on. Margot is sitting nearby, looking out of the window.

"Problem?" asks Ms. Clooney as she stops at Margot's desk.

Margot shifts her gaze to her book. "No problem," she says.

I wait for Margot to look up at me and roll her eyes, but she doesn't and I feel the earth shift a little beneath my feet.

For eighteen months, Margot and I have been best friends. For eighteen months, since I moved to Blair, Margot and I have shared secrets and laughed at the losers and sighed at the crapness that is our lives. Before I came along it was just Margot and Desi. Then it was Margot and El and Desi. The magical power that is three.

But lately something's changed. It may not be real, but it's there like a tiny stone in my shoe. I limp along as if I have no choice, but I could make it more comfortable in an instant. I just need to confront Margot, but what do I say? "Are we still friends? Have I done something wrong?" I can see her eyebrow lift now as if asking whether I've gone crazy.

Maybe I have.

35.

It's the geography field trip day and I've forgotten to bring my signed form, so I secretly sign another one and hand it to Mr. Ray. I have not been looking forward to this. I figure the constant waves breaking in my stomach are due to an early start and no breakfast.

We get on the minibus and everyone is jostling to get the seats at the back. Desi and I choose a seat in the middle and Sarah sits in front of us and turns around. I feel rather than see Dylan pass us to go farther toward the back of the bus.

"I've made up some forms for you and Dylan to use—you know, for the whole stats thing."

Desi nudges me but I keep a straight face and say, "Thanks, Sarah."

"I figure if it's okay with you and Dylan I'll just take some photos and maybe interview some people. Stats really aren't my thing. Did I mention that already?" asks Sarah.

"Yep."

"I've also brought my digital camera. You know, for my part of the project. But you can have it if I finish early."

"I don't think we'll need a camera . . . Thanks anyway, Sarah."

When we get there, everyone piles out. Dylan, Sarah, and I group together and Sarah reads the riot act about what we should be doing.

"Here are the forms," she says. "It's probably better if you split up—we'll finish earlier that way."

Our group is responsible for taking stats around the mini golf club and shopping plaza across the street. They flank a busy road that seems filled with trucks. I feel sorry for the little cars. Sarah leaves to record interviews with some sales assistants and shoppers and golfers. Dylan stands with the form in his hand and looks lost.

"I'll take the stats for the number of cars in and out of the parking spots," I say. "You note the number of trucks and buses going past."

I try not to think about the last time he saw me.

Dylan heads off to the corner, clicker in one hand and Sarah's form in the other. Mr. Ray checks on us a couple of times and nods encouragingly.

"Remember to note the vegetation surrounding the area," he says. "Native or introduced?"

Vegetation? I guess you could call the mini golf green vegetation. There are houses on either side of the plaza and golf course, but they are old row houses and don't have a lot of front garden space. I notice a tree here and there, trying to exist among the fumes. A gray house has some ivy twining in and out of its chain fence and I note it under the section for introduced species. The convenience store has a pot of something green out front but it's pretty wilted and I don't know if I should mark it down or not.

It's a busy place. I'm amazed at how life goes on when we are locked away at school. Trucks arrive to deliver supplies. Mothers come and go with tribes of children—one kid comes over and leaves his grubby paw prints on my school pants. A man with a haircut meant for someone much younger pulls up in a red convertible.

All the while, through these comings and goings, I watch Dylan out of the corner of my eye. Sometimes I think he is watching me. I wish it were Eric instead. In a perfect world it would be Eric standing on the corner. If it were Eric standing there, I could go over and discuss the project. We could talk about other things. Find out what we had in common.

But it is not a perfect world.

Sarah finishes early so I get her to take photos of whatever vegetation she can find. Then Mr. Ray blows his whistle and Dylan comes over to wait for the bus.

"I think we are definitely going to get an award for this project," says Sarah. "Group photo." She bunches the three of us together, holds the camera at arm's length, and clicks.

I'm in the middle, between Dylan and Sarah, and my head only comes up to Dylan's shoulder.

36.

That afternoon I get home from school to find Mom home already. I ask her what's wrong and she mumbles something about leaving early as she shuffles around the kitchen. I'm not really listening. My head's full of my own problems as I grab a bowl of cereal and head to my bedroom. Half an hour later I'm lying on my bed with my earbuds plugged in when Bella thumps through the door. She's wearing a scowl that could wilt full-grown trees.

"What?" I ask, removing one earbud.

"You lazy cow," says Bella. "Are you going to be a leech all your life?"

Wow, you seem upset.

I hate to see you like this.

Is there something I can do to make you feel better?

Also, am I a cow or a leech?

"Shut up," I say, as I put the earbud back in.

But Bella pulls both earbuds out.

"When are you going to grow up, El? You treat this place like a hotel. I'm sick of sharing a room with you—you're a pig. There's no housekeeper to clean up after you anymore. Mom's not home to pick up your slack—"

"Well, whose fault is that?" I snarl.

"It's not Mom's," she says.

But I don't want to hear it. I blame Dad the most, but I blame Mom too. She should have been keeping an eye on things. The word "bancrupt" flits around my mind like a mosquito. I swat it away but it returns.

"Sick . . . lazy . . . bed . . . drugstore . . . medicine . . . dinner," are Bella's words that filter through to me.

"What? Slow down. What are you talking about?" I finally manage.

Bella's lips are a thin grim line. "Our mother is sick," she says slowly. "That is why she is home from work so early. So you need to get your lazy butt off that bed and make dinner while I go to the drugstore for some medicine. Got it?"

Then she leaves before I answer. I wait until I hear the door slam before I creep into Mom's room. Her blinds are down. She takes up hardly any space in her big bed.

"Mom?" I say.

She answers with a coughing fit. "Looks like I have your cold, Ariel," she says finally, with a shaky laugh.

Great, so it's my fault.

She reaches out to me, but I pretend not to see.

"I'm going to make dinner," I say.

Mom always used to make dinner.

When Dad had his own business, Mom would go into his office every weekday, but she would always be home when we came back from school. She'd have a snack for us. Make sure we were warm enough, cool enough, happy enough. She'd sit down and help with math. And listen to our funny stories. We might have had a cleaning lady, but it was Mom who sewed our concert costumes and read *The Little Mermaid* to us and chased out the shadows when there were monsters in the middle of the night.

And now I'm making dinner. And my mother is in her bedroom. And I know I should chase out the monsters in her shadows, but I just don't know how to do it.

I make chicken with instant gravy, which is the only thing I know how to make apart from noodles and eggs. I hate dicing up the raw pink meat, so

I throw it in the frying pan quickly to keep bad thoughts away. The hot oil spits and catches me as I push the meat around with a wooden spoon. The mark on the inside of my wrist is white-hot with pain. Instead of feeling angry or sad, I feel satisfied.

This is what I deserve. I am a lazy cow-leech.

After dinner, Bella spreads out her textbooks on the dining table. Mom is back in bed, after sitting on the couch and watching a little TV. She is asleep when I poke my head into her room, so I don't disturb her. I go into my bedroom, shut the door, and take a good look at the room. It's looking like a before and after photo, all in one. Bella's bed is neat, her bookcase is tidy, and her shelves are full of interesting things.

My side of the room is the before picture. By the time I finish with it, over two hours have passed. I'm humming along to my iPod—the last present I got before the B word ruined everything—as I put the final touches to the bedside table that Bella and I share. I get an idea and sneak outside to the communal garden, if you could call it that. On my way back inside, the cat lady next door appears at her door calling for Socks or Shnookums or whoever.

"A bit chilly out," she says.

I just nod as I sidle back inside.

When Bella comes to bed, she bends down to sniff the stolen flowers sitting bravely in a small glass of water. She doesn't say anything about the room but climbs into bed, reads a while, then turns off her light.

"Night night," she mumbles.

And the knot in my stomach loosens just a little.

Later on, when Bella is snoring quietly and Mom has stopped coughing from her room, I creep into the bathroom and dial Leonard's number. He calmly lets me know that his hours are from 10 a.m. to 7 p.m., Monday to Friday, but that if it's an emergency I can call his cell phone. Then his answering machine beeps and waits for my message and I hang up.

I find my way to Mom's room, stand in the doorway, and listen to her breathe.

37.

As I settle down to another session of Radio SRN on Wednesday, Margot and Desi give me sad little waves through the tiny window that looks out onto the hallway. Then they walk away. When the door opens, I expect to see the vice principal. Instead it's Dylan—the last person I want to see. Dylan is now taking up 80 percent of the space in my little radio booth. A work folder dangles from his hand.

I figure Dylan is here to talk about the geography project.

"Can we do this later?" I ask.

"Listen, I just want to say . . . ," he begins. "About the Eric thing . . ."

If he's going to remind me that Eric is taken, I don't want to hear it.

"I'm busy," I say.

Dylan just closes the door behind him and leans against the wall.

"Go ahead," he says. "Don't let me stop you."

I shuffle the papers, trying to get them in some order, and gasp when he grabs my wrist.

"What are you doing?" I hiss.

I watch, mesmerized, as he traces the outline of the oil burn on the inside of my wrist.

"What happened?" he says. He seems angry.

"Cooking," I say, pointedly looking at my wrist.

He finally lets go, but doesn't look convinced that that's the real story.

I'm not sure how to demand that he leave without sounding desperate, so I shrug as if it doesn't matter and start the announcements. Halfway through I hear the door click shut behind me and I sense that Dylan has left. I'm not sure why, but I feel disappointed.

Today's pile of announcements just goes on and on. Missing uniforms, lost textbooks, an invitation to join the debating team. To save myself from being bored I try a few different accents. This keeps me amused for a while. The last paper in the pile is a notice about the school newspaper.

"Don't forget, Blair students, you can volunteer your talent to this year's school newspaper—articles, fiction, illustration, and photography. Meetings are every Monday at lunchtime in the Library Conference Room."

I switch off the system and tidy up the notices. There's a scrap of paper on the floor and I pick it up, but it's not a notice. It wasn't on the floor when I first arrived. I crumple the page and throw it in the garbage. There's still ten minutes of lunch break left—enough time for me to eat my limp sandwich from home.

I don't know why, but something makes me stop at the door, grab the crumpled sheet from the trash, smooth it out, and put it in my pocket.

38.

Angelique stops by my locker that afternoon and I try to ignore Margot's exaggerated thumps as she loads up her books for home.

"Hey, El," says Angelique. "You're doing a great job on SRN."

"Thanks," I say. Neither Margot nor Desi has said anything about what I'm doing except to offer suggestions of how to get out of it.

"Eric told me you helped him out with that basketball court time thing—"

I wave her into silence and hope that Margot hasn't heard.

"It was nothing," I say.

"I wondered if you'd like to come to the game Friday night? The guys have to win this one to have any kind of chance of being in the finals. It should be good."

I can feel Margot's eyes burning into me, and my laugh is shaky.

"No can do," I say. "Friday night is movie night."

I suddenly remember that Angelique saw me shopping with Mom last Friday night and I hope that she doesn't mention it.

A little frown forms between her two delicately plucked eyebrows and she lays a hand on my arm.

"That's too bad," she says. "It would have been fun."

Margot makes some more noise with her locker, then walks off, her bag slung over one shoulder. She turns around halfway down the hall and says, "Did I mention I can't make it this Friday night, El? Feel free to go to your basketball game."

Angelique looks uncertain. "Hey, your friends are invited," she says. "The more the better."

"Thanks anyway," I say, wondering whether I should run after Margot.

The stone in my shoe stops me from running.

That afternoon I make my usual visit to Leonard. He seems distracted, sad almost, and I want to ask him what the trouble is, but really that's his job, not mine. When he says hello, I try to add a little warmth in my return nod.

Outside in Leonard's park, the trees are finally

bare. They stand bravely in the weak winter sunlight, but they look lost. I want to hug one as I leave, but I don't want Leonard to see me and think that I'm crazy, so I just touch their trunks as I walk past.

That night Desi calls me to thank me for passing on my cold. She'll be in bed for days, she says cheerfully.

"You know how my mother is," she says. "I've already had enough chicken soup and lemon drinks to sink the Titanium."

"*Titanic*," I correct her automatically.

The thought of Desi's mom fussing over her sick daughter is making my heart shrink. It's hurting.

"Maybe you could come over on the weekend," she suggests. "I'll be climbing the walls by then."

I leave her with the idea that this is going to happen, then I call Margot. I have an awful feeling that she's not going to talk to me, but she gets on the phone and I tell her about Desi.

"That girl is a hypochondriac," she says.

I just laugh. Desi is Desi.

"Of course, it's quite a coincidence that we have that science test on Friday. I'm sure she's devastated about missing out on that," Margot drawls.

"About today," I say.

There's silence on Margot's end. I picture the thin line of her mouth.

"About Friday night . . . ," I begin again.

"Yes?"

"Are we going to the movies or not?"

"I told you," says Margot. "I have other plans."

"Oh." I want to ask what those plans are, but something in her voice tells me the subject's off limits. "So what movie does this remind you of?" I ask, trying to get a laugh.

"It's not the end of the world if we miss a movie night," says Margot briskly. "It's not like we're joined at the hip or something. I do have other friends, you know. It's not like we come as a two-for-one package."

I want to say something snarky but my voice is strangled in my throat, so I hang up. I play back the conversation in my mind. I wonder who Margot's other friends are because, well, frankly, I've never met them.

I pull the crumpled scrap of paper from my school pants pocket. I smooth it out and study it.

It's another piece of artwork from Dylan. This time there are no flames or spiderwebs.

The sketch is of a girl with wide eyes and a puzzled expression. Her face takes up the whole page. There is no room for hair—her chin finishes somewhere off the page. Each eyelash is clearly defined. There is a smudge of shadow under each eye.

It's really pretty good.

Dylan has added his signature to the bottom left-hand side of the paper.

I shove the paper into the bottom of my drawer.

39.

The next morning, Eric and some other guys are jogging around the track. As I stand watching, Eric waves. When I tell Angelique at the lockers that I've changed my mind about coming to the game, she seems pleased. She is surrounded by a group of girls giving me the once-over. Some of them are from the newspaper.

"I'm so glad you can come," she says.

Then she scribbles her address and cell phone number on a scrap of paper.

"If you can get to my place by 6:30 we can go together."

I want to ask her what she'll be wearing, but I feel a bit stupid.

"Wear something warm," she warns, as if reading my mind. "The gym can be freezing."

Being with Angelique is confusing. She is the girlfriend of the only boy who has made my heart melt. She is my enemy. She is a person who can't decide what to buy when she goes shopping. I want to look out for her. She's warm. She's really smart. She seems to like me. And I can't help but like her.

What's not to like?

I've left the lockers behind when I hear someone race up behind me.

"El, wait."

It's Angelique and she's wearing an apologetic smile that makes me think she's changed her mind.

"I just wanted to say . . . When you meet my father, if he mentions anything about me being at your place last weekend, can you just agree? Cover for me?"

"Red jacket," I mumble.

"What?"

"That was you on Saturday. In the red jacket."

"Saturday? Yes, I was there Saturday. Did you see me?"

"I thought so."

"So you'll cover for me?"

"Sure," I say. "Did you rob a bank?"

"I was visiting my brother, Tony. It's just that Dad and Tony aren't really talking at the moment. I'm not supposed to be speaking to Tony either."

"No problem," I say, then Angelique leaves.

My idea of who Angelique is keeps changing.

Margot's not at the lockers first thing and she doesn't make it to class. I'd been worrying about seeing her but suddenly I'm worried that she's not around.

At lunchtime I call her. I smuggle my phone out of my locker into the bag with my lunch because we aren't supposed to have phones at school.

I try Margot's cell phone number then her home number but there's no answer. I toy with the idea of calling Desi at home, but I don't have many minutes left and should probably save them for an emergency. Why can't I be on an unlimited plan like everyone else?

I take Angelique's scrap of paper and add her information to my phone's contacts list.

And I wonder for the fortieth time what I am going to wear on Friday night.

40.

Before I go to Angelique's, Mom and I have a fight. I can't find anything warm to wear that looks good, so I make do with a summer top and a scarf.

"Don't be ridiculous, El," she says, dumping groceries on the kitchen table. "You're just getting over a cold." Then she has a coughing fit.

"I don't have anything else," I say. "I'm warm enough."

"Warm enough in here," she agrees, then coughs again. She has only had one sick day off this week. Maybe she should have taken more. I have an image of her funeral and my heart begins to hammer in my chest.

Are you okay?

Are you really sick?

I don't say these things.

Instead, Mom and I snap and bite at each other until finally Bella agrees to lend me her new jacket if we'll just be quiet. She also lends me some money for the game and we both know that I'll never pay it back. Mom disappears into her room and comes out all dressed up. She looks good. She's wearing more makeup than I've seen on her for a long time. I'm dying to ask where she's going—she hasn't been out for so long—but I won't give her the satisfaction of me talking first.

"I'm going out," is all she says as she heads for the door. "Do you need a lift to work, Bella?"

Bella shakes her head. "Jackie's picking me up."

Jackie is Bella's friend from our old life. She has lots of friends that she still sees, even after the BANKRUPT thing.

Bella gives Mom a quick hug and frowns at me as she passes by.

"I need a lift, Mom," I say, then add, "Please."

I give Mom the address and she seems to know how to get there, and I realize that it's near our old Big House. I still don't ask her where she's going or who with. I don't get a chance. She's too busy giving me the third degree about who, what, when, and why. When she finds out this is Angelique's house, the girl she met in the shoe store, she seems satisfied.

We finally pull up at a large white mansion with

black wrought-iron gates flanked by white lions. Normally Mom would have something to say about this type of house design, but she just asks, "How are you getting home?"

"Angelique," I say.

"Do you have your cell phone?" asks Mom. "Call me if you get stuck."

"Thanks for the lift," is all I say. Then I slam the door and don't wait for her to drive away. I hear the car leave, its distinctive chugging loud in the still early evening as I press the doorbell. I'm feeling a little nervous, because I'm half an hour early. I hate to be late.

Chimes ring out five times before Angelique finally opens the door.

"Commin," she says, slurring her words as she stands aside to let me in.

I'm embarrassed. Is Angelique drunk? She stumbles up the white hallway, which I think might be marble. I follow her into her bedroom, not knowing what else to do. I'd figured at least a couple of her friends might be hanging around, but the house is quiet.

Angelique has a large bed with a silk duvet cover and lots of pillows in shades of blue and white. In one corner of her room, which is about as big as my home, is a corner desk with a Mac laptop, printer, and scanner set up. A corkboard is dotted with pieces of paper: invitations, notes, a phone number. There's a TV in another corner and a shaggy white rug in the middle of the room. There aren't any posters on the wall. Maybe she isn't allowed to have them.

"Are we still going—?"

Angelique cuts me off with a high-pitched giggle, which comes out of nowhere.

"Dad's not home. We're gonna have to catch a taxi." She sways a little. "Oh, shit." Then she crumples in a heap at my feet.

I think back to all the movies that I've ever watched with drunk people in them.

"Jelly beans," whispers Angelique, and I think she's lost it. "Jelly beans," she insists, and points to her bedside table.

I open a couple of drawers and find a half-empty package of jelly beans. I hold them up. "These?" I ask.

She nods and I pop one into her mouth.

I fumble for my phone and dial 911. Then I ask her for Eric's number.

"Don't call Eric," she pleads. "You can't tell anyone."

I want to call Mom, but Angelique is holding on to my hands like she is drowning. I ask her what I should do, but all she can say is, "Just stay. Just stay with me."

"I'm not going anywhere," I say.

41.

I've never ridden in an ambulance before. I'm
sitting in the front and there's an EMT guy in
the back with Angelique. He's setting up a drip or
something and it's all very *ER*. The driver quietly
whistles as he steers through the traffic. He does
this for a job, every day, saving people. I want to
give him a medal for being so calm and together.

When we get to the hospital, they whisk
Angelique away and I walk to the emergency room
reception window and wait in line.

The carpet leading up to the reception desk has
a well-worn track—a track made by thousands of
hopeful, fearful, ill people before me. The scent hits
me before I reach the woman behind the desk. The
sweet smell of perfume—musk—barely masks the
smell of antiseptic and stale air-conditioning. My
stomach flips a warning and I hope I'm not going
to puke.

"The doctor will be with you shortly." The

broad, starched desk guardian with the bristling mustache tells me. She sits in her glassed-in reception area safe from germs, vomit, and the stench of fear. The scent of musk is strongest here. I wonder if there was a special on, like maybe 80 percent off. Her skin has been scrubbed raw and it gleams pinkly under the harsh light. Pink piggy skin that has me thinking of a pork roast. Her blunt left hand strangles a pen.

I go back to my uncomfortable plastic seat in the waiting room.

A young guy opposite me gives a wan smile, his nose a smashed watermelon. No pits. An older man sitting with him catches my gaze.

"Football practice," barks the older man, laughing. His nose also wanders over his face. His breath cuts through the musk, alcohol tainted, with an underlying smell of tobacco. The nicotine-stained fingers of his left hand drum a restless tattoo on the seat next to him. The sign opposite him says No Smoking.

"Christ, we're gonna be in for it from the old duck." He laughs, nudging his son in the ribs.

I'm guessing he's talking about his wife. I wonder if she looks like a duck. I think it's very rude of him to mention it. My mind seems to be wandering away from what's really happening.

Somewhere in this concrete maze is Angelique. She is probably wearing one of those sterile white gowns that gapes at the back. Her army of followers has no idea where she is. And if they did, would they choose to be here? Would they revel in the drama? The tabloid throwaway-ness of it. Or would they just find another Angelique to leech on to?

Then I wonder if Eric's basketball game has finished. Whether he has missed Angelique watching him from the sidelines. He's probably frantic. I'm worried about him but don't think it's my place to call him. Angelique made that pretty clear.

Angelique is alone in this ants' nest of nurses and doctors and aides and others all scurrying about their work. The halls are a maze of dead ends and closed doors. I can't begin to guess where they have taken her.

The desk guardian glances at me, then continues her precise printing. Her glasses are a prop to glare over.

I did not pass her test when we first arrived. I gave her Angelique's name and address. I fumbled for my phone and gave her Angelique's cell number, but I couldn't give a home number or her father's first name. Luckily, Angelique's details are in the computer. She's been here before.

I close my eyes and images of Eric and Dylan and Margot tumble over one another—a waterfall of images that make no sense.

The smell of stale coffee nudges my senses and I make my way to the visitors' cafe. Discarded stir sticks blaze a trail to the garbage can. Sugar encrusts the edge, and garbage is overflowing onto the beige carpet. Bad color choice. There are no cups in sight.

There is a drink-vending machine nearby and I feed in some coins. Nothing happens. I hit the button again and wait. That's when I notice the handwritten sign that apologizes for the machine being out of order.

I kick the machine and it feels so good that I kick it again.

I make my way back to my seat. I have made my mark here with used tissues, an unread magazine, and a stray hair clip. Bella's jacket lies abandoned on the seat as the heating turns on its tropical charm. I want to be in this seat when the guardian comes looking for me. If I stay here, everything will be all right.

The bright lights of the waiting room beat down. My head throbs and I close my eyes, just for a moment. The next thing I know I wake with a jerk. My mouth is dry and I hope that no one has seen me drooling or committing some other gross act. I check my phone—almost 9 p.m.

A woman nursing a bandaged finger has replaced the guy with the watermelon nose.

"The doctor will see you now."

I jump out of my seat, but the guardian is talking to the woman with the bandaged finger. I feel slightly dizzy and realize I haven't eaten since breakfast. It hasn't even been half a day since Mom dropped me off at Angelique's house, but it may as well have been a lifetime.

I miss my dad. I suddenly want to see his face, climb into his arms, and have him hold me steady so I won't fall.

I want to call someone. Bella's at work. Mom's out—God knows where or with who. A date? I file that thought away for later inspection. I know they would come if I called, but it seems selfish to ask.

I flip open my phone and scroll through my contact list. It is surprisingly short. Desi would be a welcome sight, but she is entirely unpredictable. Besides, she's sick. Margot? Well . . .

I scroll down further, and then back up again.

"Hey, you can't use that here."

It's a young kid with chubby cheeks. Those cheeks are so perfect and plump that I want to pinch one so that it leaves a red mark. He's pointing to my phone like it's a loaded weapon. Then he points to a sign that shows a cell phone and a large red line through it.

I stick my tongue out at him and press the "dial" button. After a lifetime of rings, someone answers.

"Hello?"

Then I break my promise to Angelique.

"Dylan," I say. "It's El."

42.

It seems like forever, but Dylan finally arrives and marches straight over to me.

"Tell me again," he demands.

He looks out of place, like a wild animal in a public park.

I give him a quick explanation as he slouches in the seat across from me. He doesn't seem surprised.

"Has this happened before?" I ask.

"She's diabetic," he says. "So where is she?"

"I'm not really sure," I say.

But Dylan's already out of his seat. He's walked over to the reception area to talk to the woman behind the glass. He moves like a jungle cat. I want to warn him that it's useless but watch in amazement as she gives him her version of a smile. He nods a couple of times then comes back to me.

"Angelique's under observation in one of the emergency cubicles."

"Can we see her?" I ask.

"Sure," he says.

I gather my stuff and stand up to go, but Dylan isn't moving. He's watching the desk guardian.

"Hello?" I say. "Can we go?"

The automatic entrance doors open and a woman and young boy rush up to the desk. The boy is crying and the woman raps on the reception window for attention. The desk guardian is trying to calm them down when Dylan says, "Now," and disappears up the hallway.

When he pushes open some unmarked double doors I'm right behind him.

"We're not allowed to see her, are we?" I pull on Dylan's arm.

"It's a free country," he says.

"How do you know where to go?"

"I've been here before," he says, and I wonder if it has anything to do with the scar on his face.

There's a nurses' station and a line of curtained cubicles—some pulled shut, some open. I think I see the lady with the cut finger, who is sitting on the edge of a hospital bed with her arm in a sling.

People in white coats and pastel-colored uniforms are bustling around. No one bothers to ask us why we are here.

"Angie!" Dylan calls out.

I swear we are going to end up in jail and I'm going to have to explain the whole thing to my mother.

"Angelique!" Dylan calls out again.

A cubicle curtain nearby pulls back. Angelique pokes her head out.

Dylan and I hurry over and shut the curtain behind us.

"Hi," says Angelique, like we're at a party.

Dylan just mumbles and sits on the one plastic seat near the bed. Angelique sits back on the bed and I'm left standing.

"El, I'm sorry about tonight. I really messed up."

"Don't be," I say. "They had your dad's number."

"I guess he had to know." She rolls her eyes. "He's going to lose it."

"Has this happened before?" I ask.

Angelique nods. "Once or twice," she says. "It happens when I don't eat properly—when I don't take care of myself."

"Do you want me to call Eric?" I ask, ignoring Dylan's snort from the chair.

Angelique shakes her head. "It's a big night for him. This game's really important."

"It's just a stupid basketball game," I say. "He'd want to be here, I know it."

I'm angry but I'm not sure who with. Angelique? Eric?

"There's a party afterward—" Angelique is cut off as the curtain twitches back to reveal a tall man in a leather jacket. His dark hair is threaded with gray and his skin looks suntanned. For some reason, it's his hands that I notice the most. His hands are slim and his fingers are long but blunt at the ends, with clean, pale fingernails. They're pulling at his jacket collar like it's digging into his neck.

"Angelique," he says gruffly. He doesn't look cross. In fact, he looks like he might cry.

"Hi, Dad," says Angelique.

Before Dylan and I disappear back to the waiting room, she introduces us. Actually, she introduces me, because Mr. Mendez and Dylan already seem to know each other. Mr. Mendez nods Dylan's way.

"Dad, this is my good friend El."

Good friend? I hardly know the girl, and we're good friends?

She gives me a hug. I don't miss the awkward pat that Dylan gives her. The sight of it causes my heart to jolt a little.

"Call me?" she asks, and I promise to as we leave the emergency room.

Dylan and I hail a taxi. He slouches in the corner

151

of the backseat and pulls out his phone. I look out the window, pretending not to listen.

"Hey," he says. "Yeah, good. Listen, Angie's in the emergency room. No, fine now. Probably a while. Maybe you should—"

He grunts a few times then says, "Whatever."

His phone light fades and we're left in the darkness of the cab.

We figure out we have just enough money for the trip to my place. When we get there we pay the driver and both get out.

"I'm off," he says, zipping up his jacket.

"Was that Eric?" I have to ask.

"They won," says Dylan shortly. "He's a little busy. Nothing he could do to help her. Thought he'd catch up tomorrow."

"I guess he's right," I say. I hate the way Dylan's lips twist. "I mean, there really is nothing he could do . . ."

Dylan just stares.

I try again. "She didn't want him to know anyway."

"Here's a tip—Eric doesn't need you to make excuses for him. Don't you get it? He's never going to be interested. You're too noisy. You have too much to say, too much attitude. And, just in case you've forgotten again, he already has a girlfriend. Your good friend Angelique." He shoves both hands into his pockets and strolls off down the road. "Good night, Ariel Ariel," he calls out.

I feel confused and hurt and angry. I want to lash out at Dylan—want to find some words that will pierce his thick skin.

Finally I yell, "Yeah, well, maybe you should mind your own business."

But Dylan's already left.

43.

When Dad left, he didn't take a suitcase. It was like he'd decided on the spur of the moment that he wasn't coming back. Mom didn't bother to gather up his stuff at first. Then one day I came home from school and I felt it straightaway. Something had changed.

With a turn of my key, the front door of the Big House (we'd already downgraded) opened, and my bag landed in the entry hall with a thump. So far, normality. The first thing I noticed was the hall coat rack. My dad's things—his golf umbrella, his jacket—were gone.

"Dad?" I called out. "Daddy?"

I waited for a reply, but the only sounds were the ticking of my grandparents' clock from the living room, the drip of a tap not quite turned off, a fly banging against a window in an effort to escape. Or maybe it just wanted some attention.

"Dad?" I repeated, as I slowly walked upstairs.

But I knew that he'd already gone.

I checked the master bedroom first. Sunlight filtered through the lace curtains, framing the dust in the air. Dad's slippers were missing from under the bed: old brown slippers with a tartan band.

The dressing table looked a little bare. Mom's things were still there, grouped on the right-hand side. Dad's silver dish remained—the one he unloaded all his coins into. The one I often borrowed from. But his comb and handkerchiefs were gone.

I opened my parents' wardrobe doors to find a gap where his clothes had been.

I poked at the hole, like I'd probe with my tongue at the space left by a missing tooth. A few bare hangers remained. His drawers were empty.

I smoothed the cover on the big bed and noticed she'd left his pillow. I hugged it to me, breathing in deeply. The only smell was the fresh smell of fabric softener. My mother had washed the sheets and pillowcases many times since he'd left.

He'd been gone for a while.

I moved on to the bathroom. Aftershave, electric razor, deodorant—all gone.

While his things had been at home, I could still pretend that he was coming back to us. That he would change his mind and we would laugh about it one day and say, "Remember the time you left?"

Well, maybe not laugh.

I moved on to the study, the TV room, the garage, the poolroom. Mom had been pretty thorough, removing any clues that he'd ever existed.

A portrait still hung on the living room wall— a picture of a family frozen in time. A tall man was holding tightly on to a chubby bald baby. You could tell by the way his fingers bit into her smooth pillowy legs that he was scared she might fall. A fine-boned woman leaned against him, her hand draped over the shoulder of a girl with long blonde hair. The woman's stance was casual, but her eyes were narrowed, perhaps in anticipation of the impending flash. Everyone was looking directly at the camera lens except for the baby. She looked off into the distance with a frown.

I studied the man closely. Clear brown eyes, a sharp nose, ears flat against his head. He seemed happy, but who could tell?

I found what I wanted in the kitchen. It was shoved right to the back of a kitchen cupboard, as if someone had tried to hide it. I grabbed it and returned to the master bedroom. I sat in the gap of Dad's wardrobe and watched the sunlight grow weaker and turn into night. Mom found me there when she switched on the light.

"Ariel," she said in her quiet voice. As if it were normal to find me sitting in a wardrobe.

I held the mug out to her. WORLD'S GREATEST DAD, it read.

"He's really gone," I said.

44.

At home in bed that night, I add another thing to my list for Leonard. It's more of a statement than a question, but I'd like to see where he stands on it.

I believe that if somebody makes a promise to stay around, like a wedding vow or something, then they should keep it or not bother making it in the first place. Because that's just crap if they leave and how can you believe anything they've said before or will say again?

45.

The next day I call Angelique's cell, but all I get is her voice mail. I mope around all morning, until finally Mom asks if I want to help her clean out the kitchen cupboards.

"Sorry, can't," I say. "I promised Desi I'd visit."

Which is kind of true.

I think about calling Margot and getting her to meet me there, but I hang up after a couple of rings. I get a bottle of soda and tell Mom I'll be home in a couple of hours. Then I walk to Desi's house. A dose of Desi was just what I needed.

I know I shouldn't be, but I'm surprised when Margot answers the door.

"Hello," she says coolly, standing aside to let me in.

"How's the patient?" I ask.

"If she's sick, I'm a two-humped camel."

We both laugh, then fall silent. I want to ask her about her Friday night, but Desi calls out, "Who is it?" and we tramp into Desi's room.

Desi is wearing pajamas, socks, a sparkly scarf, and pink earmuffs. Her room is filled with stuffed toys and posters and knickknacks that line her windowsill and bedside table.

"We were just talking about you!" says Desi, flinging her arms around me for a quick hug.

As I remove myself, I see Margot give Desi a warning look.

"You were?" I ask.

"Is that for me?" Desi says, pointing to the bottle of soda. "That's just what I feel like."

"I'll get some glasses," says Margot, escaping to the kitchen.

Then Desi launches into how sick she's been feeling, how high her temperature had got to, how bored she was.

"You realize you missed out on the science test," says Margot as she comes back in balancing glasses.

"Oh, no!" Desi pouts, looking miserable.

"Oh, no!" Margot and I say together with oversized pouts of our own.

Then Margot and I are laughing and Desi finally joins in.

"I actually studied for that test," says Desi.

"Studied?" asks Margot.

"I brought my textbooks home," says Desi.

Then we talk about nothing in particular for the next two hours and everything feels like it used to. Well, nearly. Margot doesn't talk about her Friday night. Neither do I. And Desi doesn't ask either of us.

"Do you think I'm loud?" I suddenly ask them both. Dylan's opinion of me had been niggling away at the back of my mind. "Do you think I have too much attitude?"

"Attitude?" repeats Margot, shaking her head as if she can't believe what she's hearing. "Loud?"

"Sure," says Desi. She shrieks as I whack her with a pillow. "What?" says Desi. "What did I say?"

"Do you have anything to eat?" asks Margot. "I'm starving."

We grab something from Desi's kitchen, which is an amazing treasure trove of chips, candy, and chocolate. Desi manages to eat a lot for a girl who's sick, and Margot keeps us entertained with a Hitchcock movie that had been on TV late during the week, called *The Birds*. The movie is set in a little seaside town that is attacked by birds. Lots of birds. There is a scene in the movie where the main characters are hiding, locked in their house, although they can hear the birds outside pecking at the building.

"It's classic Hitchcock," says Margot. "It's not just a movie about outside forces. It's also about the forces within us."

Desi says she knows what Margot means. She then goes on to talk about what the lead actress is or isn't wearing in *Hearts Are.*

All the while I can feel the elephant in the corner of the room.

Everyone knows it's there but no one's talking about it. I want to tell them about the drama of Friday night and Angelique, but the right words won't come. Maybe it's because I don't want Margot to turn cold and act like she doesn't care. Maybe it's because Angelique swore me to secrecy. Either way, I am stuck pretending everything's normal.

46.

I phone Angelique's cell on Sunday night and again there is no answer. Mom's still coughing her head off, so I do a load of laundry and she acts like she's won the lottery. Even Bella pats me on the cheek in a nice way, but instead of feeling good it makes me feel bad. It didn't take much effort. It's just not something I think of doing.

Cow-leech. I make myself a promise to help out more around the house, but I doubt that I'll keep it.

I call Angelique's number again. "Just checking how you are," I say to her voice mail. "It's El."

At school on Monday, Desi is waiting for me at the gate.

"All better?" I ask.

"Mom made me come, even though I am not entirely well." Desi coughs for dramatic effect.

The school bell rings as we make our way to the lockers.

"I hear Angelique and Eric had a fight on Friday night," says Desi, shoving at the books falling out of her locker.

"Where did you hear that?"

"In the bathroom, this morning. I think it was Amanda Bingley. I had the door shut so I can't really be sure. Anyway, she said that Angelique didn't turn up to Friday night's game."

I'm guessing by now that Margot has told Desi that I was invited to the game by Angelique. I bet my friends are both dying to know what really happened. If they just asked I might tell them.

"Maybe Angelique had a good reason," I say.

Desi shakes her head and grabs my arm. "The beginning of the end, I'd say. Angelique out, El in."

I know she's wrong but I feel a little warm glow inside.

"Angelique's nice enough, but I just don't think she's Eric's type," says Desi.

At lunchtime I check out the conference room but Angelique's not at the newspaper meeting. Coop, the newspaper's self-designated sports reporter, waves and I half wave back and move on to the biography section. The chat today is all about the latest episode in Margot's sister's on-again off-again relationship with a loser named Rufus.

"I mean, Rufus?" says Margot. "How could she go out with a boy named Rufus?"

"Sounds like a dog," says Desi. "Ruf ruf."

We move from Rufus to science and I realize that I haven't done my science assignment that needs to be handed in at the end of the day. Margot and Desi give me some good excuses, but Margot goes too far when she offers her excuse of a dead grandmother.

"Don't say that, Margot," says Desi, looking around. "That is such bad luck. What if El's grandmother dies tonight? How would you feel?"

"I would feel pretty amazed, considering El's grandmother died ages ago," says Margot.

Then Margot rolls her eyes at me and I think how good it is to have someone who knows everything about you. Someone you can share your best and worst secrets with. Then I realize that I have been keeping secrets from Margot, and it makes me uncomfortable. Suddenly I want to come clean. To tell her everything.

"Can I come over tonight?" I ask Margot.

Margot shakes her head. "I'd love that, but I've got some serious studying to do if I'm going to pass that entrance exam for advanced math."

"You're taking advanced math next year?" I ask.

Margot looks like she's been caught doing something illegal.

"But I can't do normal math," wails Desi. "That means we won't even be together for math next year. How can you do that? You're breaking up the team. The only thing we're going to have left together is English."

Already the guidance counselor is on our case about making the right subject choices for next year. It seems Margot must have been listening after all.

At the end of the day it takes me a quarter of an hour to explain to my science teacher, Mrs. Van der Droop, that I did in fact do my science assignment but that I was unable to hand it in due to a virus on my computer.

"That's fine," she says. "Feel free to bring a note from your parents to confirm your excuse and you can hand it in tomorrow."

"Parent," I correct her.

On a scale of one to ten, I figure my day has rated a two. I'm stomping down the corridor making as much noise as possible when someone yells at me from behind.

"Hey, El. Wait."

It was Eric.

My day had just gone from a two to a seven.

I waited for Eric to catch up. Eric Callahan was running after me. Actually my day was a nine.

"I just wanted to thank you. For Friday night. Angie told me. You saved her life."

I shake my head. "I'm sure I didn't."

"I'm just glad you were there."

"How is she?" I ask like I'm really interested. I mean, I am interested. I am also interested in the fact that Eric's arm has just brushed mine as we walk through the school gates.

There's a rumble of thunder from far away and I hope that Eric doesn't think it's my stomach.

"She's fine. Just taking things a bit easy."

"How was your game?"

Eric's face breaks into a smile and I swear the sun has peeped out from the clouds.

I'm walking home with Eric Callahan. Actually, Eric Callahan is walking home with me, because I know for a fact where Eric lives and it is nowhere near me. Eric is giving me a play-by-play description of Friday night's game, so I don't have to say much. Sometime during our walk he has grabbed my backpack and swung it over one shoulder like it's a bag filled with cotton wool. Considering it has my science textbook, math textbook, English novel, and pencil case, I'd say it was more like a sack of potatoes.

I want to say, "Hey I can carry that," but the fact is I like that he has it. That Eric Callahan has my backpack slung over one shoulder and is walking home with me.

I ask him what he wants to do after finishing school. I figure he's going to say something to do with math. Instead he says maybe a sportscaster—TV if he can get it. He tells me Mr. Mendez pulled a few strings to get him an internship in the newsroom at ABC.

"Wow, that's so cool," I say.

"Yeah. As they say, it's not *what* you know . . ."

"Hey, you could cover the Olympics. Travel the world. You could be famous," I say.

"Yeah," says Eric. "I could cope with that."

The streets around the school are filled with old houses. Most of them are huge. Some are freshly painted and have neat gardens. A few of these have garden gnomes or other statues dotted about. Some have concrete columns and lions guarding their doorway. Sprinkled among these are houses with crumbled brick fences, cracked concrete driveways, and weeds for gardens. A woman collecting her mail eyes us suspiciously.

We take a shortcut through a back street and pass an abandoned factory surrounded by a high wire-mesh fence with litter collected at its base. A guard dog lies in the shadows.

The thunder rumbles are louder now. Leaves and trash rush around like they've got somewhere else to go. My hair whips at my face, and I feel the temperature drop even before the first fat plops of rain touch the sidewalk.

"Oh," says Eric.

And then the heavy clouds drop their load on us and we're standing still in shock.

"Come on," says Eric.

He makes a dash for a strip of trees just past the factory and I follow close behind. When he stops under the shelter of a large pine tree, I bump into him and we laugh.

"Where did that come from?" he says, but all I can think of is the wet wool smell of Eric's school sweater.

The rain is hitting the ground with so much force that it is bouncing back up. It's making so much noise that, when Eric says something, I miss it. I shake my head to show him I can't hear and he leans in closer to my ear and says, "I think we should wait."

For a moment I think he's talking about us. About maybe him and me getting together in the future sometime. In the next second I realize he's talking about the rain. I could nod, but instead I reach up to his ear and say, "Okay."

"I give it ten minutes," he says in my ear.

When I say "says," I mean he breathes the words into my ear and I shiver as his words race around my body.

"No way," I say. "At least half an hour."

He shakes his head. "Trust me," he says.

A trickle of water is inching its way down the back of my sweater but all I can think of is how I wish this would last forever.

I think I love you, Eric Callahan.

Love.

Of course I don't say this. Instead I stand next to Eric and watch as the rain pounds down. After about five minutes, the rain backs off to a slow drizzle. By then, Eric and I are standing close together sharing body warmth without touching.

"Let's go," he says.

I wonder who put him in charge, but the thought disappears quickly.

When we reach the corner of my street, I realize I do not want Eric to see exactly where I live.

"Thanks," I say, holding out my hand for my bag.

Eric hands it over.

"Well," he says.

"Well," I say. "Say hi to Angelique." It kills me to say this, but I am suddenly having a reality check. This is Angelique Mendez's boyfriend.

"Sure," he says.

As I walk down the street he yells out at me and I turn around. Eric's holding his palms upward to the sky. The drizzle has stopped.

"I told you to trust me," he says. "Ten minutes."

47.

At home I can't stay still. I definitely cannot sit down and finish my science assignment. Instead, I rush around picking things up from one room and putting them down in another. I have dinner cooking by the time Mom and Bella arrive home and they look suspicious.

"What have you done?" says Bella. Then she sniffs the air. "Is that tacos?"

I show her the jar of taco sauce and nod, my nose in the air. "Of course," I say. "Nothing but the best for my family."

"Have you been taking drugs?" says Bella.

And it's true. I am on a high. Every time I think back to my time with Eric after school, I get another kick of something that surges through my body.

I notice Mom's looking tired as she gives me a little pat on my shoulder—the kind of pat you might give a wild dog—and I wonder if that's what I've been lately. For a long time.

"You've got time for a bath before dinner, Mom—" Then I realize we don't have a bathtub.

"I might just have a shower," says Mom.

Bella sets the table with a tablecloth and a large square orange candle that has already collapsed down one side from previous lighting.

"It's the best I can do," she says crossly when I give it a once-over.

"I'll get some flowers," I say.

It's dark outside and hard to see what I'm pulling up. Someone comes down the stairs, two at a time, and I see a flash of dark curly hair and a ragged T-shirt.

"Good night, Peggy," a male voice calls out.

Nearby a cat hisses and yowls at me. I wonder if it's the cat lady's pet. She's standing outside her door with a bag of dry cat food. She's shaking it like some witch doctor warding off evil. The food inside the bag is making a racket and I think I'm going to get away with sneaking inside, but she spies me and stops shaking.

"Hello, dear," she says.

"Hello," I mumble.

She's looking at the flowers in my hand and I look down at them in surprise as if I don't know how they got there.

"You haven't seen Bolt, have you?" she says.

"Bolt?"

"My cat. Captain Thunderbolt is his full name, but he answers to Bolt."

"I think I might have heard him over there," and I wave in the direction of the bushes.

"He loves his treats," says the cat lady.

"Okay," I say. I open our door and the smell of onions fills the air.

"Now, what is that interesting smell?" she asks.

"Tacos," I say.

She makes an "o" with her mouth like it's the most decadent thing.

I'm not really sure how I invited her for dinner. I hadn't meant to. One minute she was talking about boiling up an egg for her dinner, the next she's seated at our table admiring the lopsided candle and flowers.

"Now isn't this nice," she keeps saying.

Mom, Bella, and Peggy, Cat Lady's real name, are having a nice little chat while I serve up tacos and rice. Bella has shoved the stolen flowers into a glass and they actually look pretty in the middle of the table, even though their roots are still attached. Mom's put on some old music that I haven't heard for years.

When I sit down, Mom opens a bottle of wine and pours everyone a drink.

"For a special occasion," she says, when she pours some into my glass.

We all clink glasses.

Peggy says, "To good neighbors."

Bella says, "To Monday nights."

I want to say something about Eric Callahan. Instead I say, "To tacos."

We all look at Mom, waiting for her announcement. She gives a little smile then raises her glass high.

"To my wedding anniversary," she says.

This is what happens: time stands still.

Well, not all time. The music continues to play softly in the background. It's a song I remember singing to in the car when we were all together. Dad, Mom, Bella, and me. The Marini family. Peggy looks confused. Bella looks like she's tasted something bad and wants to spit it out. But Mom looks serene.

You can't celebrate a wedding anniversary if you're not married anymore. I mean, get with the program, Mom.

Of course I don't say this. Instead, time speeds up from where it left off and Mom says, "Two, four, six, eight," which is her version of saying grace at the dinner table.

"Dig in, don't wait," Bella finishes off, though her voice is low.

"Now isn't this nice," says Peggy.

I shove a forkful of rice into my mouth so I don't have to answer.

"By the way, Ariel," says Peggy, and I silently curse Mom for introducing me as Ariel, "your friend dropped by on Sunday."

"My friend?" I say.

"The pretty girl. Dark hair," says Peggy, picking at her food like a bird.

"Sunday?"

"We were out grocery shopping," says Mom.

"I asked her if she wanted to leave a message, but she said not to bother," says Peggy.

"That's okay," I say. I think I will call Angelique tomorrow night if she isn't at school tomorrow.

Then Mom and Peggy talk about curtains and everything is normal again.

In bed that night, all I want to think about is Eric. Eric in the rain. Eric carrying my bag home from school. Instead, I think about Mom. And wedding anniversaries. And how much I hate Dad.

Dylan Shepherd pops into my head, then the upstairs man—Angelique's brother, Tony—turns on his shower and the water pipes bang loudly as the hot water kicks in.

I get up for a midnight trip to the fridge. On the way I pass Mom's room.

"Happy anniversary, Mom," I whisper.

48.

The next day, I get a lunchtime detention for not handing in my science assignment and not handing in a note to explain why.

Desi thinks this is really harsh, but as I explain to her, there is a little more to the detention than a late assignment.

"I think it was the 'whatever' factor," I explained between classes.

"The 'whatever' factor?" asks Desi.

"When Droopy said she'd be deducting five points for each day the assignment was late, I said 'whatever.'"

Desi groaned. "You're lucky she didn't slap you."

"Whatever," I say.

We giggle all the way to the next class.

In geography, Mr. Ray gives us the lowdown on our second field trip. There is a general buzz in the air. Not because we love geography so much, but the thought of escaping school is making everyone happy. Make that most people. When I look at Dylan sitting at the back, he is balancing a pen on one finger and looking out the window.

"Poor Margot misses out," says Desi.

"That'll teach her for getting into history," I say dryly.

At lunchtime I head off to the coffin room. I consider not going, but I know that this could end up causing even more trouble, so I just go. The place is packed. There must be some group detention situation going on because it is almost standing room only. The only seat left is at the back, two tables away from Dylan Shepherd. I wonder why he is here and think that maybe I'll ask him. I settle myself then lean forward to give him a smile, but he just stares at me. It's like he doesn't even know me. I sink back into my seat.

Note to self—first impressions do count. Bored. Macho. Thick.

The fact that I'd turned to him for help not that long ago left my cheeks burning with shame. I spend the entire session keeping my head down and not making eye contact with anyone. I make a list of things to do after school.

1. Call Angelique

2. Finish my science assignment

3. Visit Margot if I have enough time

When the bell rings, I scoot out the door, but Dylan is lurking in the hall and catches me as I go past. Other bodies push past me, forcing me to stand beside him out of the way.

"She's okay," says Dylan, his eyes burning into mine.

"Angelique?" I say.

He gives a curt nod.

"I tried calling her." It sounds lame.

"I just thought you should know," he says.

Then he disappears up the hall and I'm left feeling ashamed. Then I feel angry.

When I get to my locker I make a decision. I grab my phone and call Angelique. After three rings, she answers and sounds happy to hear from me. We talk a bit, I promise to visit her, then I head off to my next class. I slip into the room just as Mr. Graham, my teacher, is sliding the door shut. I have escaped a late pass by seconds. Desi and Margot are sitting together and I dump my books on the desk next to theirs and smile.

"Whatever," whispers Desi.

And we laugh.

It turns out that my science assignment only takes a couple of hours after school. It's amazing what I can do when I put my mind to it. After I finish, I ask Mom for a ride to Margot's house.

"How will you get home?" she asks. "I don't want to go out twice in the car."

"I'll get a ride back," I say.

I toy with the idea of taking my school clothes and staying the night, but it's a weeknight and I know Mom won't be up for it. As Mom drives, I realize that I haven't checked whether Margot will be home. Maybe I should have called first?

Then I think about all the things I need to tell her, including the hospital drama on Friday night.

"What movie does that remind you of?" I hear her asking.

Or maybe not.

Mom drops me off at Margot's gate and I wave as she leaves.

As I get to the front door, it opens and Steph says, "Oh hi. Margot's in the dining room." Then she walks to her car and I close the front door behind me.

"Margot?" I call out.

I walk up the hallway and notice that the dining room door is slightly ajar.

What I see makes no sense.

49.

Eric and Margot are bent over a textbook. As I'm standing there, Eric points at the page with his pencil and Margot nods. Then he gives her shoulder an encouraging squeeze. She smiles.

"Hello?" I manage.

They look up. Eric looks a little confused, and Margot gives me her bored look.

"Eric's helping me with advanced math," she explains.

"Hi, El," says Eric, and smiles. Then he looks at his watch. "Is that the time?" He shoves a book, some pens, and a calculator into his backpack. He picks up a white envelope off the table.

"Sorry, Margot, gotta run," he says. "See ya later, El."

He slams the door behind him.

And that's when it hits me. I guess I always was a slow learner. I'm not sure whether to laugh or cry or what. Margot has seen that I know and she tries to walk away but I grab her arm and spin her around to face me.

"How long?" I demand.

She looks at me. The bored look has left her face.

"Eric's been giving me extra help. With math. Just a couple of weeks—"

"How long have you liked him? How long have you liked Eric Callahan?" I demand.

Then she doesn't try to pretend. I give her points for that. She raises her chin a little.

"A while—," she begins.

"How long?" I shake her arm.

She just shakes her head.

"You've liked Eric Callahan for 'a while' and you never bothered to tell me? Never once bothered to mention that while I was gushing over him—going on about how cute he was, how smart he was, how utterly perfect—you wanted him too." I try to grasp what was now the truth. Had always been. "But you used to say he wasn't your type. Boring. You said he was boring."

Margot shrugs.

"You just let me go on and on . . . You were laughing at me! You were just taking your time, just waiting for the right moment, then," I snap my fingers, "you're going to snap him up. My God! What kind of person are you?" I back away from my best friend, Margot—make that ex–best friend—as she reaches out to me.

"I never wanted to feel this way," she says lamely. "I wanted to tell you. I came to talk to you on Sunday, but you weren't home. I needed to—"

"Angelique! What about Angelique?" Suddenly I'm sorry for the girl who has everything. I look at Margot's clothes and she's wearing her regulation red and black, her bird necklace. "Do you know he likes pink?" I say with a strange laugh. "Maybe you could accessorize in pink—"

"Eric doesn't know," says Margot.

"You're pathetic," I say. "You make me sick."

Then I run outside just in time and I really am sick. I throw up behind a well-trimmed hedge, then I throw up again. All the bad, confused thoughts and feelings have finally found somewhere to escape. At one point I feel Margot's hand on my shoulder but I shrug it off.

"Get lost," I say.

It's a long walk home.

50.

When I get home, I grab the phone and slink into the bathroom. I call Leonard's office and listen to his answering-machine voice. Then I dial his cell phone number and wait. He picks up at only four rings.

"Hello?" he says. "Hello?"

I want to say, People let you down, Leonard. Just don't trust anyone 'cause people let you down. Fathers, friends, the whole world if you let it.

Instead I say, "Sorry, wrong number."

I don't want him freaking out that he's got someone suicidal on the line.

I hang up but feel slightly better. We may have a strange relationship but Leonard is never going to pretend to be my best friend and then go off with my boyfriend.

Leonard is never going to make promises and break them.

That's the thing about Leonard—he is solid.

51.

I start hanging out with Angelique. Just like that. One day it's the three amigos and then there's only two. Desi stands by Margot, which is fine by me. Mind you, she looks miserable. Every now and then we come face-to-face and she says, "Hi, El" and then walks away quickly. I don't blame her for being loyal to Margot. I wonder if she knows the truth about Margot's secret crush on Eric, but I doubt it. I wonder what lies Margot has told her.

Margot, on the other hand, is being a total bitch. In class, she keeps close to Desi and as far away from me as possible. Outside class, she looks through me, like I'm nothing—no, less than nothing.

Life with Angelique as a friend is different. I'm not sure how I got here. Suddenly I'm in the high-profile crowd. I have a lot more numbers in my phone. Her friends are nice enough, but the in-jokes I had with Desi and Margot don't exist in this life.

I follow Angelique's friends' cue and start calling

her Angie. Angelique's friends are more like my friends at Regis.

There is Laura, whose pale skin and red hair make her look like a model.

There is Tess, who is short, pretty, and sweet. Everyone wants to look after Tess like she's a little pet.

There is a couple I call the Katrina twins, though they're not twins and only one of them is called Katrina. They look so much alike, I can only tell them apart if they are together. I am sure they were separated at birth.

Then there's Jessy, who's loud and funny and who doesn't like me much. I can tell she doesn't like me by the way she watches me when I talk to Angelique—sorry, Angie.

And then there's Eric. I get a chance to see a lot more of Eric these days.

I'd been thinking about what Dylan had said—about how Eric would never go for a girl like me. But I could change—I know it. So Eric doesn't like loud girls. No big deal—I don't have a lot to say right now.

I get through my second geography field trip with Dylan and his number counter. Sarah is off somewhere with her camera taking pictures of who-knows-what. I have a clipboard and feel like a total loser with Dylan a few steps away from me. We have to work closely together. Our job is to write down how many cars use our part of the road, including a breakdown of buses and large trucks.

It's so boring that after a while I say something just to break the monotony.

"So," I say.

"So," he says.

"How's your number counter going?" I ask.

"Okay."

He starts with "yes" or "no" or "okay" answers, but I keep talking and soon he joins in and we're having a conversation. He tells me about his little brother. I tell him about my big sister and her fast-food chicken job. He tells me his grandfather used to be a sign painter. I say that might be where he gets his talent from. He tells me about his last school and I tell him about mine. We don't mention Eric or Angie.

"So why did you move?" I ask.

"I had issues with the old school," says Dylan, pressing his clicker as a large bus lumbers past us. "Some people I could do without."

"Oh."

"It doesn't matter anyway. I'm getting a job as soon as I graduate."

"What do you want to do?" I ask.

Dylan shrugs. "Anything."

"You could do something with your art—you're pretty good." I remember the artwork sitting in my drawer at home and feel embarrassed.

"That's just kid's stuff. Art isn't going to get me anywhere," says Dylan gruffly.

"Who says?"

"My dad," snaps Dylan.

I'm thinking that Dylan's dad might have it wrong when a car squeals around the corner. It's going way too quickly to take the turn properly and ends up clipping a parked car as it goes past. The noise is an awful crunch and then there's another squeal as the car takes off down the road.

"Hey!" I shout.

"What an idiot," says Dylan. "We should call the cops. Did you get the license number? Hey, are you okay?"

I'm suddenly shaking so hard that I drop my clipboard. I laugh but it turns strange. Crying once in front of Dylan was bad enough. Twice would just be pathetic.

Dylan touches me briefly on the arm.

He picks up my clipboard and starts to tell me a joke about a dog and a cow and an exploding house. The joke doesn't make sense, but I finally stop shaking and laugh anyway.

"Hey, you two. Are you working or what?" It's Sarah waving to us from across the road. I burst out laughing again.

"That girl is a control freak," Dylan says.

52.

Most Mondays I hang out with the school newspaper group. Sometimes Dylan drops in when he's not in detention. Angelique is after him to do some illustrations for the newspaper, but he's playing hard to get.

"My stuff's no good," he says, but we all know he's lying. Even he does.

Angie wants me to write a review of my top five movies for the year. I stall and say maybe, maybe. I haven't been to the movies for a while—it reminds me too much of the three amigos. Three friends that went their separate ways.

On Wednesdays, I do my stint on Radio SRN, but I don't do anything out of the ordinary. I don't want to sound like I'm showing off or anything—so I've quit the multiple accents and funky music intro. After school on Wednesdays I visit Leonard and we don't say much.

On Friday nights I go to the game with Angie

and we cheer on Eric's team. Sometimes Dylan comes along, sometimes not. I don't like the Friday-night Dylan. I prefer it when he's not around. Even when he's not looking at me, I know he's watching. Watching for me to make a move on Eric. As if I would. I just need to be around him. Maybe I should have explained that to Dylan, but probably he wouldn't believe me.

Not being into sports, I'm surprised how quickly I get sucked into the excitement of the game. There's a lot of yelling and banging feet when something exciting happens and I want to join in. Instead I copy Angie's polite clapping. Sometimes Eric is so psyched up after a game, he ignores Angie. He's so busy thumping his bag and kicking it around when he loses, or high-fiving his teammates when he wins, that Angie just waits on the sidelines until he's ready. It's not Eric's fault that he ignores her. I want to push her forward, but Angie is content to wait.

Afterward we grab something to eat, unless it's really late. Dylan never sits near me—we're always at opposite ends of the bench. When we go to the food court I sometimes catch a glimpse of Desi and Margot, but it's like I'm seeing an old movie rerun that doesn't make sense anymore. They never look my way but I feel them watching me anyway.

On Friday nights, Mr. Mendez always gives me a ride home. The first time he took me home, he seemed a little angry, but after that he was okay. Maybe it had something to do with me living near his son.

Angie and I exchange stories. The Mendez family is Angie, her father, her brother, Tony, and her mother, who lives in France. Her brother and father aren't talking.

"Dad is strict," Angie explains. "Tony blamed Dad for Mom leaving. Dad and Tony had a big fight. Dad wanted Tony to apologize, but of course . . ." Angie shrugs her shoulders. "Dad told Tony if he didn't apologize, he had to get out. So Tony left. I think Dad thought Tony wouldn't leave. I think Mom sends Tony money sometimes."

"Do you miss your mom?" I ask.

Angie shrugs. "We were never that close. She was always busy. I'm closer to my dad. But I am going to see her during the summer—maybe you could come?"

Oh, yeah. That was really going to happen. Maybe two years ago, but not today. Not unless Angie was paying.

"Is your mom really a model?" I ask.

Angie nods. "Was."

"So do you want to be a model or a journalist when you graduate?"

Angie shrugs. "My father wants me to be a journalist."

"And what do you want?' I ask.

She shrugs again.

One Tuesday, about a month after the breakup, we get our grades back for our geography project. Sarah has done a great job of desktopping it. Our stats have been turned into bar graphs, and her historical input includes some old photos from the Internet. She's done some nice interviews with the mini golf players, who complain about how the traffic fumes interfere with their game. Candid shots appear on every page, including the photo of the three of us.

We get high marks for the project. I put a copy in my underwear drawer. Mom finds it there when she puts away my clothes that night.

"That's that Nice Young Man," she says. "You should invite him over again soon."

"That's my geography project," I snap. "A-plus."

"Good work, El," she says with a funny little smile on her face.

The next day I say to Leonard, "This is just a waste of money."

He shrugs. "It's my money," he says. And then he looks like he wishes he hasn't said anything. He writes something down in his notebook. He'd better not leave me alone in his office again. I'm dying to find out who I am according to Leonard. Or maybe not.

That night, when I ask Mom what Leonard meant, she explains that Leonard had taken on my case pro bono.

"Do you know what that means?" she asks.

"I know what it means," I say. "For free. A charity case. God, how poor are we?"

Mom continues cutting an onion. Bella flashes me her shut-up glance as she walks past, but I can't let it go.

"How much longer are we going to live here, anyway? I mean, when's it all going to be straightened out?"

"It *is* straightened out," says Mom dully.

"So what are we still doing here? How much money did we end up with?"

"There is no money," says Mom.

I know it's the truth. Somehow I've known all along, but I need to hear it anyway.

"What do you mean?" I ask.

Mom puts down the knife and spreads her hands. "El, you know about the bankruptcy. There's just nothing left. I know I led you to believe . . . I thought that . . . Your father—"

"Yeah, well, he's really left us in the shit, hasn't he? You lied to me. You said this was only temporary." I wave my hand around the tiny kitchen and dining family room. "What about all our furniture? What about all my things?"

"It's in storage," says Mom. "I suppose I should sell it—"

"And school? Don't tell me I'm stuck at crappy Blair till twelfth grade. I need to get back to my old life."

"But you have new friends now. And you can still have your old friends."

"Don't be stupid, Mom. That wouldn't work. Me at Blair and them . . ."

"Bella's kept in touch with her friends. Nothing's changed. She still goes out."

"They're at college. She's lucky. And Leonard. What about Leonard? Why has he taken me on for free? Am I some kind of guinea pig? Is he some kind of pervert or—"

I see it coming before it happens, but I can't

believe she's going to do it. Mom slaps my face and I stop talking.

"Jesus," says Bella, then a door slams and she is gone.

I stand looking at a stranger who has tears in her eyes. She reaches out to me and I flinch away. Then I go to my bedroom and lie down on my bed. In my mind I take out my secret jewel—my walk home with Eric. It's starting to look dull, but I take it out anyway and give it a polish and look at it from different angles.

Although my door is shut I can still hear the sound of Mom crying in her bedroom.

53.

Mom's left for work by the time I get up the next morning. She's made me lunch and I grab it and chuck it in the garbage. It lands with a delicious thump. A thought jumps into my head and I say it out loud, trying it on like a new piece of clothing.

"I am a beaten child," I say. "I have suffered child abuse," I say a little louder.

"I'll give you child abuse," says Bella, who has been watching me from where she is drying her hair in front of the wall heater.

"You saw her. She slapped me. I should call the police," I say.

"She was wrong. But you . . . you need to grow up, El," she says. "Asking her all that stuff. What did you think was happening?"

"I just want it to be like it was. I want to wake up and find everything back to normal."

"This is our normal now. Get used to it."

"Mom's never hit me before."

"Well, what do you expect? Talking about furniture and school, as if that's what matters. And trashing her boyfriend like that—"

"Boyfriend? Since when did she have a boyfriend? I didn't say anything about a boyfriend."

"Well, friend."

"What friend?"

"Leonard," says Bella.

"Leonard!" I repeat. "Leonard. What about Dad? And isn't Leonard married?"

"Divorced."

"Oh."

I need to talk about this with someone right away. Not Bella, because she's acting like it's all normal. Not Mom, obviously. I could call Angie, but I'm not sure that she would get it. The whole hugeness of it. She'd probably be nice to me, but I feel the need for some straight answers from someone who knows the whole story.

I call Margot's cell phone. She's the only one who can help me. Before she can answer, I hang up. I decide to text her instead. Somehow it's easier to write it than to speak it. My mind races as I consider the possibilities of my new situation. It takes me three attempts before I get a message that works.

MOM'S NU BFRIEND IS MY LEONARD. SHE SLAPPED ME. WHAT WILL I DO? xEL

Already I feel better.

My good feeling doesn't last long. By the time I get to school it drops away like the floor of an amusement park ride beneath my feet.

A bunch of Angie's friends (I still think of them as that) gather around me, patting my arm and cooing like a flock of pigeons eyeing a bag of scraps.

"Are you okay, sweetie?"

"Hey, he wasn't worth it."

"Are you still talking to her?"

I drop my bag and raise my arms so that they fall back a little.

I'm panicking that maybe Dylan has been blabbing about my crush on Eric.

"What are you talking about?" I ask.

"We got your message," said Jessy. Even she looks concerned. "About your mom and Leonard—your Leonard."

"Oh. Holy—oh." Little bits of information trickle into my brain, like the first thawing of a frozen stream.

"I mean, we didn't even know you had a boyfriend," says Jessy.

"Oh," is all I can say again. Then I pick up my bag and head for the bathroom.

I am still sitting on a toilet-seat lid when the bell goes for first period.

This is what I have worked out so far:

A. I have sent a group message to everyone in my phone's contact list about Mom and Leonard.

B. People in the list include Angie, my mother, my sister, Leonard and Eric and Dylan, to name just a few.

C. By now there is a rumor spreading around the school that my mother has just run off with my boyfriend.

D. Eric thinks I have a boyfriend.

E. Dylan thinks I have a boyfriend.

F. By now there is a rumor spreading around the school that my mother beats me and the vice principal is probably contacting Children's Services as I sit here thinking.

The bathrooms are probably my second-favorite place to be at Blair. Now, school bathrooms are usually disgusting, but the principal has this thing about cleanliness. I know this because there's always a notice for Radio SRN about keeping the school clean and tidy. The fact that he offers a cash prize at the end of each term is enough incentive for students to give it their best. I've seen kids grab garbage out of the trash cans and take it to the yard monitor, just so they can get points for the end-of-term garbage tally.

The tiles in the girls' bathrooms are yellow. Not an abusive yellow, but a nice mellow yellow of morning sunshine. Some are cracked, but the grout between them is white. The school janitor cleans the toilets twice a day. They smell like lavender—in a bathroom kind of way. The best time to be there is when everyone else is in class. Sometimes I get a pass to go to the bathroom, shut the door, and just enjoy the quiet dripping of the taps.

I am still running through A, B, C, D, E, and F when Desi finds me about twenty minutes into first period. When I say Desi, I mean her hand. I'd know that hand anywhere.

"El?'" she says.

I want to say something, but my voice just makes a little squeak. The next thing I know there are two hands waving under my door.

"Open up, El," says Desi.

I sag with relief. By the time I open the door I hear the machine-gun clatter of Ms. Clooney's heels enter the bathroom.

"Omigod," says Desi.

"Well, well," she says as she rounds the corner. "Do you girls have a pass? No? I didn't think so. See you at lunchtime detention—today."

"I guess we're even now," whispers Desi.

54.

I get through the day without any further interruptions. I sit by myself in class, though Desi keeps looking at me like a mother hen might look at a stray chick. Lunchtime detention is non-eventful. I sit alone at the back corner of the room, and Ms. Clooney lets me sit there, away from prying eyes.

At the end of detention, Ms. Clooney says she has some good news for me. I doubt it, but I listen politely. She tells me she has submitted my detention story to the school newspaper and that it has been accepted for the end-of-year publication.

"Okay," I say.

I don't even bother getting angry that she has done this behind my back. I wonder why Angie hasn't mentioned it. I head for the door, but Ms. Clooney stops me.

"What are you doing with your life, Ariel Marini?" she says.

"What?" It was the cat-and-mouse game with a twist. Just me and Ms. Clooney and no one watching.

Ms. Clooney looks me long and hard in the eye. For once I look back at her, really look, and I see a person. Just a person with washed-out gray eyes.

"I don't wish to see you in detention again," she says quietly.

Then she goes and I'm a mouse left without a game.

At the end of the day I check my phone and there are eighteen messages. I scan through them. Bella's says I should be banned from using technology and was I all right. There is a message from Mom that just reads "sorry." There is no message from Margot. This hurts more than any slap on the face.

The days roll on.

Mom and I are civil to each other. She has told me sorry about thirty-seven times and I've said sorry too, but I spend a lot of time in my room. I curse the fact that we don't have Internet access at home, but then reconsider and think maybe it's just as well no one can instant message me. In the end I get so bored I do my homework. That's when I know that I've reached an all-time low.

I don't go to basketball that week. I tell Angie

that I have a headache, then I sit at home and watch a rerun of a classic chick flick called *Sleepless in Seattle*. This gives me a chance to cry without anyone asking questions. It actually turns out to be not a bad night. Mom has been given a box of chocolates, I don't ask by who, and we sit on the couch together and watch TV, eat chocolates, and argue about the ending.

Then Bella gets home from work and the three of us watch the next movie—some Elvis movie—and though Bella groans through all the corny lines, she has us up twisting and rocking and rolling and we laugh together like we haven't laughed in years, until Mom collapses against the door frame and says, "Oh, that's enough. I have to go to bed. Good night, you two."

I wait for her to kiss me on the forehead, but I haven't let her do that for ages, so I just say, "I think it's cool."

"What?" says Mom.

"I think it's cool that you're going out with Leonard."

Mom looks bewildered, like she's opened the door to the wrong house.

"We're not going out, Ariel," she says. "He's just someone I can talk to."

Then she kisses me on the forehead, goes to her bedroom, and shuts the door quietly behind her.

On Sunday, Angie drops in. She's been visiting her brother and seems happy.

"How's your headache?" she asks.

"Headache . . . oh, yeah. Fine, thanks."

"I should introduce you and Tony one day."

"Yeah, that would be good," I say. I can think of a few things I'd like to say to him. Him and his water pipes.

"I just wanted to make sure you were all right."

"I'm fine," I say, still embarrassed about the group text message.

"El, someone told me something on Friday . . . something that I need to ask you about."

A tap has turned on in my stomach. A trickle of cold water is slowly filling me up.

"Sure," I say. "What?"

"It's Eric," she says.

I can't believe Dylan has done this. It suddenly occurs to me to wonder why Dylan hangs around the basketball group.

"Someone told me you have . . . that you're interested in Eric."

Surprisingly, I'm very calm. "Who said?"

"It doesn't matter," says Angie. "Is it true?"

"Yes," I say. I feel embarrassed. Like I'm at an AA meeting and I've just stood up and said, "My name's Ariel Marini and I have a crush on Eric Callahan."

She nods her head slowly. "I just wanted to ask you. I wanted it out in the open between us."

I laugh and it's a little shaky around the edges but I manage to pull it off. "Doesn't every girl at school have a crush on Eric Callahan?" I ask. "He *is* the most gorgeous guy in school."

She lays a hand on my arm. "Are we okay?" she asks. "This is really awkward."

"Are you crazy?" I pull a face. "Eric Callahan is your boyfriend. Yours. There's no way I'd interfere with that. Besides, there's someone else I'm into now. Your informer was a little behind in the news."

Angie looks relieved and asks me who it is, but I shake my head and change the subject. She tells me she tried out for the school play and got the lead role.

"Hey, that's great," I say. "Is it a musical?"

Angie shakes her head. "*Romeo and Juliet.*"

"Fantastic."

"I don't know. I've never done a real drama role before."

"You'll be great. What does Eric think?" Oh,

good one. I'm trying to convince Angie that Eric isn't on my mind and he's the first thing I talk about.

Angie doesn't seem to notice. She just shrugs.

"He thought it was a bit, you know, lame."

"Lame?" I echo.

"Eric's not really into the whole theater thing, if you know what I mean. It's going to be taking up some of my Friday nights."

"So?"

"So that's our night. Eric needs me at the game. He says I keep him focused."

"Focused," I repeat. "But you'd be great."

"I was in the Future Players Theater Company for a while. Did I mention that? I never got a part, but it was fun selling tickets at the door and helping backstage."

"So why did you stop going?" I ask.

Angie just shrugs. She's looking so lost I change the subject. I tell her that Mom and I are at least talking politely to each other, and what started out as an awkward moment turns into an okay afternoon.

Before Angie leaves for home, I stop her at the door and ask her casually how she and Eric got together.

"Dylan," says Angie. "Dylan and I went out for a little while about a year ago. We were in the Future Players together. He used to paint the sets. He was really sweet."

"Dylan?"

"But we weren't really going-out material."

"Then he introduced you to Eric," I finish off.

Angie nods. When she leaves all I can think of is one thing.

Poor Dylan.

I nearly forgive him for telling Angie.

55.

Sometime, late, late on Sunday night, an idea gets into my head and won't leave. I struggle to find the word, but it takes a midnight trip to the fridge to crank my gears.

Hypocrite.

I, Ariel Marini, am a hypocrite.

I have ranted at my best friend for having the secret hots for a boy I like. I have abused her and shunned her and had some awful thoughts. I even threw up in her mother's perfectly manicured shrub. But I am doing exactly the same thing to my supposed friend Angie. Well, not exactly.

If there's a movie for this, I don't know it.

I bet Margot would, though.

56.

The next Wednesday I don't go to my Leonard appointment. I feel bad, but I can't bear to see him—not after the texting fiasco. I guess that he will probably tell Mom, but I don't know what else to do.

On Friday night Mom drops me off at Angie's, and Eric's waiting there. Suddenly I'm conscious of the pink top that I'm wearing. I've resurrected it from my bottom drawer. I don't know why I've worn it. I feel like I'm on the edge of knowing something but there's a little way to go and it's around a corner so I just have to keep traveling.

"Angie's not coming," Eric says as he opens the door.

"Is she sick?" I ask.

"I really need her there tonight." Eric is frowning. "But she says she needs to rest."

I find Angie in her bedroom, lying on her bed.

"Hey," she says.

"Are you okay?"

"I'm a little worn out. I'm gonna take it easy tonight."

"I'll stay then," I say, sitting on the edge of the bed.

But I don't want to stay. I want to spend the night watching Eric weave his magic on court. I want to sit across from him at the food court and watch the way he jokes with the guys and drinks his milkshake and pushes away the lock of hair that is always falling over his face.

Angie says she wants an early night. She insists I go to the game. All the time I'm thinking that it's wrong to go, but then there's a knock at the door and Eric and I leave to catch our ride.

Eric and I sit together in the back of Coop's dad's car. Coop is the tallest player on the team. On court he is like a graceful gazelle. Off court he's a daddy longlegs spider, all arms and legs. And his face turns red whenever he talks to girls.

"Where's Angie?" asks Coop.

"Sick," says Eric. He sounds pissed, like Angie's ruined his night on purpose.

Coop is folded up in the front seat but keeps turning around to talk to Eric. Eric leans forward, and he is taking up a lot of space. Every now and then he turns to include me in the conversation and I join in, but mostly I'm content to listen and feel his warmth down my left side.

Sometime during the conversation Eric mentions that the boys' basketball team needs more court time and maybe I could take it to student council.

"Right," I say. "Right."

But the idea leaves an ice cube in my stomach.

Coop's dad drops us off at the main entrance. Eric is helping me out of the backseat when Dylan appears out of nowhere.

"Where's Angie?" he asks.

I stumble as I get out of the car, aware that he is watching me.

"Sick," says Eric. "Again. Let's go, Coop."

Eric and Coop rush off to the locker room, which leaves Dylan and me staring awkwardly at each other.

"She's tired," I explain further. "Otherwise I would have stayed with her."

Dylan nods curtly and moves off ahead of me. I feel like I've been judged again and a spike of anger makes my arm shoot out and grab Dylan's shoulder to spin him around.

"She wanted me to come," I snap.

"Sure, she did," he says.

He is standing there looking so smug, looking so damn superior, that all I want to do is wipe that look off his face.

"I know," I say to him.

"You know what?" asks Dylan.

He kind of looms over me, but I'm not scared. In fact I feel totally in control.

"I know about you and Angie. How you went out. How you introduced her to Eric. It kills you, doesn't it? Kills you to see them together—"

Then suddenly I'm run over by a truck.

I'm slammed into a wall.

I'm crushed by an elephant.

What I'm trying to say is that Dylan kisses me. I think it is Dylan, I mean, it probably is, but my eyes are closed and I am thinking, "Do your eyes naturally close when someone kisses you, and can it be a real kiss if they don't?"

And I am thinking, "I think he just drank some Coke."

And I am thinking, "Is it possible that I have just melted into Dylan Shepherd and he has melted into me so that we are just one person?"

And I am thinking, "Help, I'm running out of breath," when finally he breaks away, and my lips are instantly feeling cold and lonely.

"You don't know anything, Ariel Ariel," is all he says.

But he says it lightly and he has that little lip curl thing happening and suddenly I am the most confused person in the world.

57.

I watch the game and Dylan doesn't come near me. A group of us end up at a nearby ice-cream place afterward, and the players go through a play-by-play description of the game, as if none of us had just watched it. The lights are dim and we're squeezed into vinyl bench seats.

Eric sits right next to me, but Dylan sits farther down the bench. My heart has been racing since our kiss and I think I may be in danger of having a heart attack. I don't look at him because I'm too scared to see his face. Everyone's excited because they won their game and are now set to play in the finals next week. There's lots of table thumping and loud laughter and Eric grins at me continually. At one stage there's a food fight and I end up with ice cream on my new pink top. Eric casually grabs a napkin and wipes away at the mess before I have a chance to do anything. He is busily talking to someone else, but I can feel Dylan's stare and my heart thumps faster.

We finally get up to leave, but Dylan is nowhere to be seen. I wonder when he left, but as I'm stepping into the cool night, he comes up and says, "I hope you get everything you wish for, El."

And he doesn't say it in a mean way or sarcastically, but is kind of humble, very un-Dylan-like and I want to rewind to that kiss and start again from there.

But Dylan's gone and the next thing I know I'm being pushed into Coop's family's car and Eric's sitting beside me. Coop and his father are reliving the game in the front seat and I'm suddenly aware that Eric has his arm resting along the back of my seat. I give Coop's father directions to my home, then I sit on the edge of the seat.

"Relax." Eric pulls me back. "You look really nice tonight, El," he says.

Then he kisses me.

There is no truck. There is no wall. There is no elephant crushing the wind out of me.

As he kisses me I think with amazement that this is my second kiss of the night.

Then I think that his lips are really wet and loose. When he tries to force his tongue into my mouth, I clamp my teeth shut and he has to be content with my lips.

I think, "Eric Callahan is kissing me," but all I feel is disappointed.

I break away, push him back, and say, "What about Angie?"

He rests his forehead on mine and shakes his head a little. Then he moves around to my earlobe and starts to nibble on it. This sets up a whole chain reaction in my body that seems to have its own ideas.

"Angelique?" I repeat.

He stops nibbling, then pushes his hair away in that manner that I find so cute. "I know, I know," he says, shaking his head.

Then he dives in for another kiss, and this time I'm annoyed.

"You know *what*?" I say.

"Angie." He shakes his head. "She's a really great girl, you know? But we just don't . . . it's just not working anymore. She's so serious. And you're so much fun."

Then the car stops and I'm home. I thank everyone for the ride in a shaky voice and walk inside on rubbery legs.

My dream has just come true and it was not what I expected.

Not at all.

58.

I blame that stupid pink top.

59.

I spend the entire weekend like a lone shipwreck survivor. I'm breathing, I'm walking, I'm eating, but I'm wondering how I survive. The one thing that had kept me going for these past eighteen months, the one shining light in my life, was suddenly dull. In fact, it wasn't so much dull as grimy. Eric had taken something pure and beautiful and turned it grimy.

Eric Callahan, *my* Eric Callahan, would never hit on his girlfriend's friend. Especially when his girlfriend was sick in bed. My Eric Callahan would never badmouth his girlfriend while trying to nibble another girl's ear. That's when I figure out that my Eric Callahan doesn't exist. My Eric Callahan was an idol that I had endowed with amazing qualities, none of them particularly real.

And I know it's not his fault, I know it's not fair, but I'm really very disappointed in him.

And what was with Dylan? Just when I think I've figured him out, he proves me wrong.

The world has turned crazy.

I sleep a lot. The world is crazy so I sleep. I think things might make sense when I wake up. But they don't, so I sleep again.

I know Mom is worried, but I can't go through it all with her. Bella is studying hard for her economics exam, so I don't want to burden her.

Burden.

That's what I was.

I was the extra luggage that you take on vacation when you've packed too many clothes. I was a burden.

I was trying out the idea when the doorbell rang on Sunday afternoon. I waited for Mom or Bella to answer it, but no one did and the bell kept ringing away.

"Is someone going to get that?" I yell out crossly, but there is no answer.

Finally I get off my bed. I shuffle to the door in my fluffy slippers, past Bella with her spread of books on the dining room table and earbuds in. As I turn the doorknob, I wonder if Eric is on the other side. I hope that it is Eric. There are a few things I'd like to say to him.

It turns out to be Cat Lady.

"You haven't seen Bolt, Ariel?" she asks.

"No, Peggy, I haven't," I say.

Peggy looks like she might cry.

"He hasn't been home since last night," she says.

She lets out a strangled sob and I pat her shoulder awkwardly.

"Maybe he just wanted to party all night," I say.

"He's never stayed out all night before," she says with a hiccup.

Somehow I find myself promising to help look for him. First, I change into some real clothes and put on some shoes, then Peggy and I go outside and look under hedges and shrubs and cars.

"What does he look like?" I ask.

"He's black," says the cat lady, "and he's got little white paws and a white chest. And he's wearing a collar. I think it's red . . . now isn't that silly, I can't remember if it's red or blue."

"Bolt! Bolt," I call, feeling a little stupid.

"Captain, Captain," calls out my companion.

We're halfway around the ground floor, when someone joins us. It's a young guy with black hair.

"Has that cat gone missing again, Peggy?" he says.

"Oh, Tony. Captain Thunderbolt is such a naughty boy," says Peggy.

I figure out that this is Angie's brother. He has

the same tall, dark looks of Angelique and the same serene aura. So I introduce myself, then the three of us wander around and look for the stupid cat. Twenty minutes later, Angie turns up and joins in the hunt. I don't have time to feel awkward. Peggy's starting to hyperventilate, and I'm worried that I'm going to have to call an ambulance if we don't find the cat soon.

Angie is the one to find Bolt. She looks up a tree to find a petrified cat sitting out on a very slender limb.

"Hey, kitty, hey," she coos.

Between Tony and me, we get the cat down and Peggy is scolding and patting the cat all at once. Somehow we all end up at my place and Mom appears from out of nowhere to put on the kettle and Bella clears the dining room table and we all sit down. It turns into an impromptu welcome-home party for Bolt, who is looking very regal and cool now that he is out of the tree.

Angie and I nudge each other as Bella and Tony strike up a conversation. I want to tell her about Friday night, but this isn't the time to do it. In fact, I'm not exactly sure what I'm going to tell her.

"The boys have made the finals," is all I say and she nods. "Are you feeling better?" I ask her.

"I'm fine. Really."

"What do you think of Dylan?" I ask. "I mean, I know you two went out . . ."

"He's gorgeous," she says. "Really nice. All tough guy on the outside but marshmallow on the inside. He really likes you."

I push her. "Shut up," I say.

"He does," says Angie. "Haven't you seen the way he looks at you? And he keeps turning up at basketball games. What's that about? He never used to come to watch."

"Was he the one that mentioned I had a crush on Eric?"

She looks confused for a moment. "What? No, it wasn't Dylan."

"Oh." My world has just shifted again. "Then who?"

"That girl—Desiree."

"Oh." I don't know what to think. "About Dylan, do you know how he got his scar?"

"Scar? I didn't realize he had one."

Then Tony says he's got some food upstairs and he's going to cook us his famous pesto linguini. He opens the door to find Mr. Mendez about to push our doorbell.

"Papa," he says.

Inside the apartment, our voices fall silent. Angie looks frightened, so I grab her hand and squeeze it hard.

"Anthony," says Mr. Mendez gruffly, with a brief nod.

Tony brushes past without saying a word.

"Angie," barks Mr. Mendez.

"Coming, Papa. Sorry . . . I need to . . . it was nice meeting you," she says awkwardly to Peggy, giving the cat a final pat.

Mom is at the door trying to get Mr. Mendez to come in, but he stands firm and says he has to be somewhere else.

"Call me," I whisper to Angie.

"An actress," Angie whispers back, getting up to follow her father. "When I graduate I want to be an actress."

And I realize Angie has answered my question from ages ago.

"I'd love a cup of tea," says Peggy from out of nowhere, and Mom puts the kettle on again.

60.

Tony calls a little later to say sorry but he didn't have some of the ingredients he needed for the pesto. Could he cook it another night? I say no problem. I also want to say a few other things like, Why don't you and your dad make up? But then I realize I'm probably not the best person to push this. In the end, Mom whips up spaghetti and meatballs and Peggy stays for dinner. Peggy tells us stories about the old days and she makes Mom laugh a few times.

When Peggy leaves, Mom gives her a peck on the cheek and a hug, which squashes the cat a little.

"Peggy's a gem," says Mom as she locks the door.

"She reminds me of Grandma," says Bella.

Mom does her still-body thing. I'm holding my breath waiting for something to happen. Waiting to find out what the rules are here.

Mom's shoulders sag a little.

"I miss her," says Bella.

Mom nods as tears spill down her cheeks.

Somebody sobs and I realize it's me.

"I miss her too," says Mom, and she holds out her arms.

Somehow we end up in a group hug.

It's a safe place to be.

61.

That night, my bedside clock says it's 11:37 when I creep out of bed and rustle around in my underwear drawer.

"Whaddya doing?" complains Bella.

"Shhh," I reply.

Bella turns on the bedside lamp and I find the paper I'm looking for. It's Dylan's sketch. I want to talk to him, to be near him, and this is the closest thing.

"What is that?" demands Bella.

So I explain. I tell her about Eric and Angie and Margot and Dylan. I tell her about Dylan's kiss and the last curtains of sleep sweep away from her face.

"Give me that," she says. Bella holds the paper under the light and studies it carefully. "Wow."

"He says his dad wants him to be a plumber or something. But I think he should do this. Something to do with art."

"He has real talent. He's really captured who you are, not just what you look like."

"What are you talking about?"

"This is you, El," she says.

"What? No . . ."

Bella drags me up from the bed and sits me down in front of our mirror.

"Look at the picture," she says.

"Yeah, so?"

"Now, look in the mirror."

I look in the mirror. Then I look at the sketch and touch the face.

"But she's beautiful," I say.

"Don't get a big head," says Bella. "Can we turn off the light now?"

62.

On Monday, I feel more like myself than I have for a really long time. The thing that gets me out of bed in the morning is not Eric Callahan. It's not even Dylan Shepherd. The thing that gets me out is . . . well, me. I feel like I've been living underwater. I check the calendar and realize what's looming but I still have to decide what to do about it.

At school I start a petition for more court time for the girls' basketball team. Mr. Nemo, our head gym teacher, argues that the boys are in the finals and the girls are not. I argue that the girls would be if they'd had more court time. We argue back and forth until Mr. Nemo agrees that he will take it up at the next staff meeting.

If he thinks I'm going to forget about it, he has another thing coming.

I see Eric in the hall a couple of times, but my heart has stopped doing its little melting thing.

Just like that. I figure he's going to be really pissed off when he finds out about my petition, but that's just too bad. He'll probably think it's personal, and it is. I have to do what feels right and this feels right.

Eric never called me after that kiss. Maybe he'd already figured it out.

On Wednesday I try some new intro music to my broadcast on Radio SRN. I'm back to my accents. I throw in some jokes. Halfway through, I nearly read out an unstamped notice, but I fudge it and put the illegal paper to one side. At the end of my session I read the notice to myself carefully, then read it again.

The words make me sad and happy and calm, all at the same time.

I'm sorry, let's talk, x Desi

I fold it and put it in my pocket.

After school, I make my way to Leonard's. First, he apologizes for dating my mother and offers to find someone else for me to talk to.

"That's okay, Leonard," I say. "Let's just keep it as it is."

Then we sit there in silence and look out the window. The trees in the park are covered in a tiny fuzz of green buds. Leonard has put on some music. It takes me a while to figure out that it's Scheme.

"That's my favorite band," I say.

"I know," says Leonard.

"Did my mom tell you?" I ask.

Leonard just points to my schoolbag, which is totally covered in Scheme graffiti.

"Oh," I say.

Then we sit and listen to the music until my session ends.

"See you next week," I say.

When I get home, Bella says, "A guy called. He didn't leave a message, but my hunch is it was Dylan."

"How could you know that?" I ask.

"'Cause I said, 'Dylan?' and he said 'Yes.'"

I hit Bella and grab the phone.

First I call Desi. The phone rings and rings and just when I'm about to hang up, she answers.

"Hello?" she says.

"Hello," I say.

"Omigod," says Desi. Then she bursts into tears and there's a lot of gulping and sniffling.

She explains that she's sorry that she told Angie about my crush on Eric, but she was just so sad. Sad about us not being friends anymore. And she thought that if Angie and I had a fight that I would come back to her and Margot and it would be just like old times again.

It was Desi's twisted logic and somehow it made sense.

Then Desi says that her mother needs to get on the phone and can she call me back and I tell her that I need time to think and we will talk again another day.

Then I call Dylan, who tells me that Angie has just broken up with Eric, so maybe I should give her a call.

"I'll do that," I say. "What a loser."

"Huh?"

"Eric. He thinks he's so cool. Sorry, that's your cousin I'm talking about."

"No problem," says Dylan. "So Friday night basketball is out?"

"I'm giving basketball a miss. Hey, why don't we go to the movies instead?"

"We?" he asks.

"Yeah, you, me, and Angie. Some other people—whoever."

"Okay," he says.

"Are you still going to go to the basketball games sometimes?" I ask.

"I dunno," he says. "No point going if the cheer squad isn't there."

We talk some more, then I ask whether he can do me a favor. Actually, two favors.

"Maybe," he says.

"First, that sketch you gave me—I was wondering if you could do a family portrait for me. We need to update the one at home."

"I dunno, El."

"Come on. You're great. Could you do it?"

"What's the second favor?" he asks.

"I want you to tell me how you got that scar on your face."

"Let's go back to the first favor," he says.

We sit on the phone talking nonsense for the next half hour. Then I call Angie but her phone goes straight to voice mail. I leave a message and promise to call again. Before I can use the phone again, Bella grabs it from me.

"Other people live here, you know," she says.

"I'm finished," I say as I walk away.

"Are you coming with me tomorrow?" Bella calls out after me. "You know it's Dad's birthday."

"Yes," I say.

"Yes, you know it's Dad's birthday?"

"Yes, I'm coming," I say.

I don't hang around to see her jaw hit the ground.

Before I go to bed that night, I make one more phone call. I call the one person who knows me the best.

"Hey," I say, when the phone goes to voice mail. "It's El. I just want to say I'm going to see Dad tomorrow. It's his birthday. I'd really like it if you could meet me there. You know the address. I'll be there at 9 a.m. sharp. Don't be late."

63.

There was a time when I was always late. It wasn't something I did on purpose. It's just that time didn't seem to have anything to do with me. It ran away while I was doing more important things. Like reading. Or watching TV. Or hanging out in my room. Bella used to say I'd be late if they were handing out $100 bills at my front door.

Then one day I just stopped being late.

Things were already a bit tough at home. We'd downsized to the Big House. Mom and Dad were fighting. I guess they both had a lot on their minds. Mom had hinted that we might have to leave our private school, so I was trying to pretend it wasn't happening. It was nearly Christmas and there was talk about no trips away and just little presents, because it was the thought that counted.

And then Gran got sick. Gran had been feeling sick for a while, then suddenly she was feeling worse. Gran's neighbor called Mom the Friday before Christmas to say that Gran wasn't getting out of bed. But Gran didn't want any fuss. This was what she always said.

"Don't make any fuss now."

But Mom had been worried and she'd taken Bella and driven the four hours to Gran's house on the Friday night. Which left Dad in charge.

I liked it when Dad was in charge. I could have anything I wanted for dinner, which meant I had take-out Chinese food and special chocolate ice cream with real chocolate chips and hot fudge the way only Dad could make it. Of course I felt sad that Gran was sick, but it was nice having the run of the house.

We each got a DVD. I got a scary movie and Dad got an old movie from the weekly specials section. He insisted we watch his movie first.

After half an hour I said, "Dad, this is strange. What's it called?"

"*Meet Joe Black*," he said.

"Who's the old guy?" I asked.

"Anthony Hopkins."

"Who's he supposed to be?" I asked.

"He's a successful businessman."

"Like you."

"Like I used to be."

"Do you like your job, Dad?"

"I love it. I have loved it."

"So?"

"So, I just need to get back on track. I've got a few deals in the pipeline. Even with the way things are right now, there are still things I can do."

"This movie's boring," I said.

So Dad put on *Down in the Deep* and that night I had a nightmare, which means it must have been a good movie.

Before he left, Saturday morning was Dad's time. That was what Dad called it, anyway. The one time in the week when he wasn't working or traveling for work or thinking about work. On Saturday mornings he put on his golf gear, had a huge bowl of muesli, then spent a couple of hours hitting a little ball around a whole lot of green grass and trying to miss the sand and the water.

Saturday mornings were also the start of my weekend. A time to sleep in. A time to watch TV in bed.

I was enjoying a rerun of a rerun of a favorite cartoon that morning when I realized I had to buy a birthday present. It was Rosie O'Connell's party that night.

I was in the middle of thinking about getting

dressed when Dad knocked on my door and popped his head in for a good-bye kiss. He was wearing his golf hat—the one that Mom had been trying to throw out for years.

"Dad, that hat is embarrassing."

"See you, sleepyhead."

"No! No, wait! I need a ride." I scrambled out of bed. "I'll just be a second."

"I'm already late," Dad warned as he left the room.

First I had to find something to wear.

Then I had to get dressed.

Then I brushed my teeth.

"Come on!" Dad yelled again from the bottom of the stairs. I heard the door slam behind him.

"Coming!"

Then I did my hair and looked for my wallet. While I was looking for my wallet under my bed, I found my lost necklace, which had a couple of knots in the chain. As I was undoing the knots, I heard the front door bang open.

"Time's up, missy. The umbrella's in the stand near the door. If you want to get to the mall, you can walk." Then the door slammed shut and I was left cursing the knotted necklace, which was now more knotted than it had been before.

He never did kiss me good-bye.

I heard the scream of tires about a minute later. Maybe it was ninety seconds. I can hold my breath for ninety seconds, and it felt a little longer than that. He hadn't got very far. I heard the tires from the end of our street just as I got the last knot out of the chain. Then I heard the dull thud of a car as it slammed into something.

I remember I tied my shoes carefully—I was worried about getting the new white laces dirty. Then I walked down the stairs. I grabbed the umbrella, but I didn't bother to open it. Already the street was busy. People were running. Cars were stopping. There was a dog in the middle of the road, chasing its tail. It came over and sniffed my fingers as I walked carefully down the road, keeping my shoes out of the mud.

I suppose I walked.

The pavement was dark and wet and oily, like the skin of a wriggling eel and steam was rising from it—the kind of steam you get when the weather has been hot and everything is still warm to the touch. I knew I could use my umbrella, but the rain had stopped and in its place was a fine mist.

Our street was in full swing for Christmas. Most of the neighbors had an unofficial competition to see who could have the most decorations. The front gardens were lined with candy-cane lights and miniature sleighs. There were some black boots, I suppose they were Santa's, sticking out of number 10's chimney, and a Nativity scene at number 14.

As I got closer to our car, I noticed something strange in a nearby tree. Someone had strung a handful of Christmas lights around the top of the tree. Pretty Christmas lights of blue and gold and silver and red. Hanging from a low branch hung a flash of red. I thought it was another light. But then I realized what it was.

It was Dad's stupid golf hat.

64.

The sky is leaden with unshed rain on Dad's birthday. There is a cool breeze and the newly covered spring branches shiver. I shove my hands in my pockets as Mom and Bella drop me off at the gate and go to find a parking spot. I wasn't sure that Margot would show, but there she is, looking her normal Margot self.

"Hi," I say.

Margot does her eyebrow lift and says, "Hi, yourself."

Thanks for coming.

I don't know how I'd face Dad without you.

I've been a useless friend—worse than useless, I've been terrible. You couldn't really call me a friend.

Just because I like Angie, it doesn't mean I like you less. You and I have history. We have fun. We like the same stuff.

The Eric thing is such a mess. I had no right to

judge you. I can see you were in a hard place. We both were.

And by the way, I just think guys are not worth the angst.

Of course I don't say any of this. I will say it, and a whole lot more, but for now I have to focus on getting through this visit.

"Thanks for coming," I say.

"I had a message on my cell phone to come here and hang out with you on your dad's birthday. So we can do that. Or we could take the day off and catch a movie at the mall. Your choice. I'm Margot," she says as she links arms with me.

And somehow I just know we are going to be friends.

"I'll give it an hour, then we'll see." We begin walking through the cemetery. "Maybe we could say hi to Gran too?"

"We've got all day," says Margot.

"Is your sister still going out with Rufus?" I ask.

"We have so much to catch up on," says Margot.

acknowledgments

As always, thanks to Maryann Ballantyne and Andrew Kelly for having faith in *Chasing Boys*. To Andrew for his insightful comments and thorough reads. To Maryann for her enthusiastic phone calls the day she finished reading it.

To Simon Lush for his help with the "ologist" scenes.

To Susie, Bernie, and Caity for reading the unedited proof and passing on their comments.

Thanks to Alison Arnold for her insistence on getting it as right as can be—including the acknowledgments. And last, but not least, Chandra Wohleber, who made sense of my English.